Addie had expected to fall asleep the minute her head hit the pillow.

She might have done just that, if there had been a pillow for her head to hit. Because, if there had been a pillow, there would have been a bed and, if there had been a bed, she certainly wouldn't be sharing it with Cole Walker.

Undoubtedly, she should be thinking of weightier issues. A brush with death should probably make her contemplate the meaning of life, not Cole Walker's lean body and the wicked charm of his smile.

Her eyes flew open as Cole shifted position slightly. Holding her breath, Addie tried to make herself as small as possible beneath the sleeping bag.

"I won't bite," Cole said quietly in the darkness.

"I know." Addie's breath left in a rush. "It's just that I'm not used to sleeping with anyone—at least not under these conditions...."

Dear Reader,

We've got six great books for you this month, and three of them are part of miniseries you've grown to love. Dallas Schulze continues A FAMILY CIRCLE with *Addie and the Renegade.* Dallas is known to readers worldwide as an author whose mastery of emotion is unparalleled, and this book will only enhance her well-deserved reputation. For Cole Walker, love seems like an impossibility—until he's stranded with Addie Smith, and suddenly… Well, maybe I'd better let you read for yourself. In *Leader of the Pack,* Justine Davis keeps us located on TRINITY STREET WEST. You met Ryan Buckhart in *Lover Under Cover;* now meet Lacey Buckhart, the one woman—the one wife!—he's never been able to forget. Then finish off Laura Parker's ROGUES' GALLERY with *Found: One Marriage.* Amnesia, exes who still share a love they've never been able to equal anywhere else…this one has it all.

Of course, our other three books are equally special. Nikki Benjamin's *The Lady and Alex Payton* is the follow-up to *The Wedding Venture,* and it features a kidnapped almost-bride. Barbara Faith brings you *Long-Lost Wife?* For Annabel the past is a mystery—and the appearance of a man claiming to be her husband doesn't make things any clearer, irresistible though he may be. Finally, try Beverly Bird's *The Marrying Kind.* Hero John Gunner thinks that's just the kind of man he's *not,* but meeting Tessa Hadley-Bryant proves to him just how wrong a man can be.

And be sure to come back next month for more of the best romantic reading around—here in Silhouette Intimate Moments.

Yours,

Leslie Wainger
Senior Editor and Editorial Coordinator

Please address questions and book requests to:
Silhouette Reader Service
U.S.: 3010 Walden Ave., P.O. Box 1325, Buffalo, NY 14269
Canadian: P.O. Box 609, Fort Erie, Ont. L2A 5X3

Dallas Schulze

ADDIE AND THE RENEGADE

Silhouette®
INTIMATE™ MOMENTS®

Published by Silhouette Books

America's Publisher of Contemporary Romance

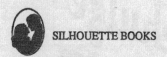 SILHOUETTE BOOKS

ISBN 0-373-07727-0

ADDIE AND THE RENEGADE

This edition published by arrangement with Harlequin Books S.A.

® and TM are trademarks of Harlequin Books S.A., used under license. Trademarks indicated with ® are registered in the United States Patent and Trademark Office, the Canadian Trade Marks Office and in other countries.

Printed in U.S.A.

Books by Dallas Schulze

Silhouette Intimate Moments

Moment to Moment #170
Donovan's Promise #247
The Vow #318
The Baby Bargain #377
Everything but Marriage #414
The Hell-Raiser #462
Secondhand Husband #500
Michael's Father #565
Snow Bride #584
*A Very Convenient Marriage #608
*Another Man's Wife #643
*Addie and the Renegade #727

Silhouette Books

Birds, Bees and Babies 1994
"Cullen's Child"

*A Family Circle

DALLAS SCHULZE

loves books, old movies, her husband and her cat, not necessarily in that order. Her writing has given her an outlet for her imagination, and she's a sucker for a happy ending. Dallas hopes that readers have half as much fun with her books as she does! She has more hobbies than there is space to list them, but is currently working on a doll collection. Dallas loves to hear from her readers, and you can write to her at P.O. Box 241, Verdugo City, CA 91046.

To Robert Rowe—my consultant on all things aeronautical. Any technical errors that remain in the story are mine. Also to his wife, my good friend Joann, in whom wit, talent and beauty are combined in one amazing package, and whose assistance in writing my dedications has been invaluable.

Chapter 1

Dying had not been on Addie's list of things to do today.

In fact, since she was only twenty-seven years old and in excellent health, she hadn't expected it to turn up on any such list for a few more decades. But as the small plane shuddered and trembled around her, she was starting to think it might be time to change her expectations.

She shot a quick glance at the man piloting the struggling aircraft but there was nothing in his expression to reassure her. Not that he showed any signs of feeling the same fear that was threatening to choke her. Cole Walker's face was still and calm, his eyes flickering between the instruments and the view outside the plane.

It certainly was a spectacular view, Addie thought. The Rocky Mountains were spread out beneath them in craggy splendor, the peaks dusted with snow. At another time, the sheer beauty of them would have been enough to steal her breath away. As it was, she would have traded all that majestic ruggedness for one nice, flat Kansas cornfield. Or maybe a good stretch of Los Angeles freeway, miraculously empty of cars.

"I'm going to set it down there," Cole said suddenly.

Addie looked in the direction he'd indicated, searching in vain for a meadow or valley or even a broad ledge—just a hint of a flat spot for landing. "It's just another mountain," she pointed out. Fear had tightened her throat, making her voice come out thin and unsteady.

"Yeah, but it looks softer than the others," Cole said.

"Softer?" she said faintly.

"Sure. It's practically a feather bed." He took his eyes off the instruments for a split second and glanced at her. His smile held a reckless edge and his dark eyes were bright and hard with challenge. "Don't look so scared. In a few minutes, you'll be on the ground, safe and sound."

"Of course." Addie forced a thin smile. She didn't doubt that he was at least partially right. Clearly, they were going to be on the ground shortly. It was the second part of the statement that she had doubts about. Safe and sound seemed more like wishful thinking than a likelihood. She sucked in a quick, frightened breath as the plane dipped abruptly downward.

"I'm going to take it down and then bring the nose up alongside the mountain," Cole explained, his hands steady on the controls.

Addie bit her lip against the urge to protest the idea of doing anything to hasten their descent. Staying in the air as long as possible sounded like a much better idea. She stared out the windshield with a kind of horrified fascination. It almost seemed as if the mountain was reaching out for them, first shouldering aside the peaks around it and then blocking out the pale blue of the winter sky until the looming bulk of it filled her vision. It didn't look much like a feather bed to her.

Cole pulled the plane's nose upward and they were suddenly skimming along the side of the mountain. They dipped lower and then lower still. There was a scraping sound and the plane shivered. Addie realized that its belly was scraping the tops of the trees.

"Put your head down!" Cole said sharply.

She threw him a quick look, saw the muscles in his forearms straining as he fought to control the plane and bring it down in one piece. And then she pressed her face against her knees and braced for the moment of impact.

Addie knew she'd never forget the sound. Logically, she knew that what she heard was the sound of metal scraping against trees and rocks, the screech of welds popping loose, but it seemed as if the plane itself was screaming in anguish. Her father would have dismissed this as the most blatant example of anthropomorphism.

I expect better than that of you, Adelaide. Use your head. You didn't inherit your mother's beauty but you did get at least a portion of my intelligence. Use it.

His voice was so clear in Addie's mind that she half expected to see him standing in front of her when she raised her head. He wasn't there, of course, and she took a moment to be thankful for that. Her father prized practicality above all things. He wouldn't approve of her being involved in a plane crash. Certainly, he'd never allow such a thing to happen on any plane on which he was a passenger. But for once in her life, she had something more important to worry about than what her father thought.

If only she could remember what it was.

A movement to her left drew her attention. Addie stared blankly at the man climbing out of the seat next to her. She knew him, of course. The tousled, dark gold hair and brown eyes were familiar, as were the solid thrust of his jaw and the deep creases that framed his mouth. She knew his name as well as her own. The thought made her frown. *That was a ridiculous saying. How could you possibly know someone else's name as well as your own?*

"Are you hurt?" His voice was deep and a little husky.

"I don't know." Her voice sounded unfamiliar, as if it belonged to someone else.

He knelt beside her and began running his hands over her body. Addie was vaguely surprised by his touch but she didn't offer a protest. She felt as if she were viewing the scene from somewhere outside herself and she was in no hurry to abandon that distance.

"I think you're okay," he said, reaching for her again. She heard the snick of a latch being released and knew it was her seat belt. "We need to get out of here."

"You're hurt," she murmured, lifting one hand toward him. Blood was streaking down from a cut on his forehead, turning the left side of his face into a garish red mask.

"I'm fine." He dismissed the injury. "We have to get out of here, Addie."

"Addie. It's short for Adelaide, you know," she offered vaguely. "I never liked that name."

"I'll try to remember that," he promised. "Can you stand up?"

"There's a lot of blood." She brought her hand up again but he caught it before it reached his face. His fingers were tight and hard around hers.

"Forget it! We need to get out of here. I don't think the plane is stable and I don't want to be in it if it heads for the bottom of the mountain."

The plane. Those two words exploded Addie's pleasant feeling of distance as surely as if he'd slapped her. She sucked in a ragged breath as memory rushed over her.

"Don't fall apart on me now," Cole snapped, seeing the sudden awareness in her eyes and the remembered terror.

"We're alive," she whispered incredulously.

Cole grinned crookedly. "Oh, ye of little faith. You can make it up to me by getting up."

As soon as he saw her start to obey, he rose to his feet and stepped toward the archway that marked the transition from the cockpit to the main body of the plane.

"Oh!" The startled exclamation brought him back to her side.

"What is it?" Nightmare visions of internal injuries skidded through his mind.

"My ankle," she said.

"Broken?"

"I don't know."

He started to kneel beside her to try to get a better look at her ankle but froze in a half crouch as the plane shivered around them. It was less a movement than a feeling of unsteadiness, gone almost as soon as it began. A warning? Addie's eyes met his. She was frightened, but there was understanding and determination there, too.

"I can make it," she said flatly. And he knew she would.

The cockpit of the Beech Craft was too small for him to be anything more than a hindrance to her so Cole backed out into the main cabin. Addie followed a moment later, hobbling badly as she tried to keep weight off her right ankle. Cole slid one arm around her waist, bracing her as they made their way across the sloping floor of the cabin. The plane had landed at an angle, forcing them to go up to get to the door. Cole worked the latch and thrust open the door, offering up a silent prayer of thanks at not finding anything jammed against it—like half a mountain. Cold air rushed in on them.

"The Rockies in January," Cole said, squinting against the late afternoon sunlight that reflected off the thin layer of snow. "Should have brought skis."

"Why didn't I think of that?" Addie murmured, forcing a weak smile in answer to the grin he threw over his shoulder.

Weak or not, at least she was neither hysterical nor catatonic, Cole thought with relief. Either one would have made the situation even worse. Not that it was exactly terrific to start with, he admitted. But he wasn't going to think about the big picture right now. It was enough to concentrate on the immediate problem, which was getting out of the plane before it decided to head for the bottom of the mountain.

Addie watched as Cole crouched and then jumped out of the plane, disappearing from sight. A thud and a smothered oath told her that his landing hadn't been perfectly smooth. Favoring her injured ankle, she eased into the opening and peered down. The drop was probably less than seven feet. Under ordinary circumstances, she could easily have slid backward out of the plane and hung by her hands for an instant before dropping to the ground. Her injured ankle seemed to throb in protest at even the thought.

"Sit down and slide out. I'll catch you," Cole said, lifting his arms.

"I'm too heavy," Addie protested, immediately conscious of the extra ten pounds she could never seem to lose.

"I can manage. Come on," he said impatiently.

Addie lowered herself gingerly to the floor of the plane and swung her legs over the edge. Cole braced himself to take her weight but found a large tan purse being dangled in front of his face instead.

"What the hell?"

"It's my purse," she said, leaning forward to peer down at him.

"I can see that," he snapped. "You actually took time to pick up your damned purse on the way out? If that isn't the most . . . female thing."

"That's a very chauvinistic thing to say," Addie admonished.

"Excuse me, *Ms.* Smith," he said, laying heavy emphasis on the title. He jerked the dangling purse from her hand and dropped it unceremoniously on the ground. "Would you mind very much getting out of the damned plane before it slides halfway down the damned mountain with your butt still planted in it?"

"There's no reason to bark at me," she muttered. She was aware that this was not exactly the time to be arguing manners but it seemed safer than thinking about how scared she was.

"Excuse me all to hell," Cole snarled. "My manners tend to get a little ragged right after I crash my plane."

"I'm sorry," Addie said, peering down at him. "I didn't mean—"

"It doesn't matter," Cole interrupted. The temper left his voice as quickly as it had entered. "Just get out of plane. Please. I'm starting to get a crick in my neck."

"Are you sure you can catch me?"

"I'm sure."

He braced his booted feet on ground churned ragged by the plane's landing and lifted his arms. Above him, Addie hesitated a moment longer, her teeth nibbling her lower lip. He restrained the urge to shout at her to hurry. She was holding together remarkably well. If she needed a few more seconds to gather her courage, it wouldn't make any difference. At least he hoped it wouldn't, he thought, glancing at the downed plane.

"Are you ready?" she asked.

"I'm ready," he assured her with strained patience.

She drew a deep breath and pushed herself away from the plane. For a split second she felt herself falling and then Cole's hands closed around her waist. He caught her easily, as if those extra ten pounds didn't matter at all. She hadn't been aware of squeezing her eyelids shut until she opened them and stared into Cole's chocolate brown eyes only inches away. He smiled at her.

"I told you I'd catch you," he said as he lowered her to the ground.

"Yes." Her smile wavered around the edges. "I'm sorry I—"

But her apology was cut short by a sudden grinding, the tearing sound as something shifted beneath the downed Beech Craft. The plane jerked and quivered, rolling toward them with all the grace of a beached whale, and then, with a sound that could almost have been a sigh, the aircraft gave in to the inexorable pull of gravity and started to slide down the mountain.

It happened in the space between one breath and the next. One moment Cole was reading the apology in Addie's blue gray eyes, the next he was staring at the rear edge of a shattered wing rushing toward their heads.

"Holy—" The oath was cut short as he dropped to the ground, taking Addie with him. He thought he heard her cry out but whether in pain or surprise, he didn't know and couldn't stop to find out. Wrapping his arms around her, he rolled away from the plane. There was a rushing, grinding sound and the ground rumbled beneath them. Cole rolled again, felt pain tear through his shoulder and rolled once more. They came to a halt well away from where they'd started, Cole on top of Addie, his body shielding hers. Off to their left, the rushing, tearing sounds continued for a moment longer and then came to an abrupt halt as the plane found a new resting place.

It was a moment before Cole moved. Beneath him, Addie lay so still that she hardly seemed to be breathing. Adrenaline pumping through his veins, he lifted his head to look down at her. Her eyes were huge in her small face.

"Better than Indiana Jones," he said, grinning.

Addie stared up at him. They'd nearly died—not once but twice. It was only through the mercy of God—and Cole's fast reflexes—that they were still alive. She hadn't even begun to think about the situation they were in, but at the very least, they were far from home free. Her ankle was probably broken, she was battered, bruised and shaken and blood was still oozing from the cut above his eyebrow. Yet he was grinning down at her as if they were having a swell time! Caught between the urge to burst into hysterical sobs and an even more powerful desire to hit him so hard that his head would spin like an owl's, Addie opened her mouth to tell him exactly what she thought of his ill-timed humor and found herself laughing weakly instead.

Cole's grin widened, his dark eyes sparkling with approval. He rolled onto his back beside her and stared up at the pale blue winter sky. His plane was destroyed, they were stranded God alone knew how far from civilization, there was a rock digging into his back and he was vaguely aware that there was something wrong with his left shoulder, but they were alive. For the moment, that made up for everything else.

He turned his head to look at her. Her face was also turned toward the sky but her eyes were closed, her lashes forming sooty crescents against the pallor of her cheeks. When she'd met him at the airport in Santa Barbara this morning, his first thought had been that she didn't look like someone who was a friend of his oldest brother's wife. Nikki Walker was sleek and sophisticated. While there was nothing ostentatious about Nikki, there was also no mistaking that she came from money—lots of it. Since Addie Smith had gone to the same exclusive girls boarding school that Nikki had attended, Cole had assumed that she would come from a similar mold.

But if there was money behind her, you'd never know it to look at her. Penny loafers, slightly wrinkled khaki trousers and matching long-sleeved shirt, a purse the size of a duffel bag, a tousled cap of medium brown curls and a face that owed none of its quiet prettiness to either scalpel or makeup—Addie Smith looked more like an absentminded schoolteacher than a woman who'd grown up in the lap of luxury. On the other hand, the Brentwood Academy for Young Women didn't exactly come cheap. And neither did hiring a private plane to fly her to South Dakota and back to pick up some cartons of books her father had purchased from a former colleague.

Nikki had recommended Cole's small charter outfit to Addie. When she'd approached him about taking the flight, he'd pointed out that it would be cheaper to take a commercial flight to her destination and then arrange to have the books shipped back to Santa Barbara, but the cost had seemed the least of her concerns.

So, here they were, a long way from South Dakota, plane crash survivors stranded somewhere in the Rockies. And she had still managed to laugh. Definitely not the reaction he would have expected from a pampered little rich girl.

"Man, what a ride!"

"Better than Disneyland," Addie agreed faintly. "I always get sick on Space Mountain anyway."

Cole's laugh was short. Euphoria was beginning to fade. They were still alive but they weren't exactly out of the woods yet, not by a long shot. Reality was starting to rear its ugly head. He sat up, catching his breath on a startled groan as pain lanced through his left shoulder.

"You're hurt!" Addie exclaimed, sitting up.

"A scratch," he said.

"How do you know? You haven't even looked at it."

"I can tell." To prove it, he rotated his shoulder and immediately wished he hadn't. He gritted his teeth and swallowed a few extremely pungent words.

"I'd better look at it," she said, her worried tone making it clear that he hadn't concealed his reaction as well as he'd thought.

"It's nothing." He was determined to ignore the throbbing pain that was making its way down his shoulder until even his fingernails seemed to ache. "I've got more important things to worry about right now," he said, looking at the Beech Craft, which had come to a halt against a jagged angle of rock that thrust out of the side of the mountain about fifteen yards further down from where it had originally stopped.

"This isn't the time to get all macho. We can't afford to ignore an injury. Not when we don't know how long it will be until someone finds us," she added, making it clear that she knew as well as he did just how precarious their situation still was.

She was right, of course, Cole acknowledged reluctantly. It wasn't as if they could hop in a car and head for the doctor. It would be stupid to let a minor injury become a major problem. Besides, there wasn't any real reason to rush to inspect the plane. It wasn't going anywhere. Even from here, it was obvious that the Beech Craft wasn't ever going to fly again. There would be time for regrets about that later.

"What about your ankle?" he asked, tacitly acknowledging that she was right about where their priorities had to lie.

"I don't think it's broken," Addie said. "It hurts, but I can move it. I think my foot was jammed against the floor when we landed. If we can find something to wrap it and give the joint a little support, it will be fine."

Cole remembered the way her face had whitened when she'd tried to put weight on her foot, but he didn't argue with her diagnosis. He didn't know what the hell he was going to do if her ankle *was* broken. His knowledge of first aid had largely been gleaned from watching reruns of "Emergency!" on television and the only thing he remembered clearly was that the paramedics seemed to spend a lot of time shining lights in the patients' eyes and then reporting that their pupils were equal and reactive. It didn't seem particularly appropriate to their current situation.

"There's a first-aid kit in the plane," he said. "There's probably an elastic bandage in it. My mother bought it when I started flying and I think it has everything but an inflatable, fully functioning doctor in it."

"Now *that* would come in handy," Addie said with a lightness at odds with the shadows in her eyes.

"Yeah. I guess she was too cheap to spring for the super-deluxe model so we'll just have to make do. Let me go get the kit and then you can take a look at my shoulder." Cole caught the uneasy glance she threw at the plane and misinterpreted its cause. "I don't think

I'm in any danger of bleeding to death between here and there.''

"It isn't that," she said. "The plane isn't likely to...blow up or anything, is it?"

Cole's brows rose. "Why should it?"

"They always do in movies. Every time a plane crashes, it bursts into flame."

His chuckle was cut short by a groan as his shoulder jabbed a protest. "When was the last time you saw someone in a movie circle the block half a dozen times looking for a parking place?"

"What?" She shot him a startled look.

"Just making the point that movies aren't always accurate." He pushed himself to his feet and smiled down at her. "Trust me, if the fuel tanks were going to blow, we'd already be toast."

Addie tried to feel reassured as she watched Cole walk toward the plane. It wasn't that she considered Hollywood a bubbling font of veracity but she couldn't quite forget all those remembered images of death and destruction following immediately on the heels of any vehicular accident, whether it was a plane or a car. It just didn't seem possible that she'd survived a forced landing on the side of mountain with no more serious injury than a sprained ankle.

She saw Cole disappear into the plane. When it neither exploded nor continued its descent down the mountain, she relaxed a fraction. When she did so, the thought struck her that the ground beneath her was uncomfortably cold. At least she could do something about that.

Walking back from the plane, Cole noticed that Addie was not where he'd left her. She'd moved to a level spot a few feet away. That great lump of a purse was beside her and she was sitting on—was that a blanket? Ignoring the pain in his shoulder, Cole quickened his pace a bit.

"Where did you get that?"

Addie looked up as he stopped on the edge of the gleaming silver blanket. "I forget what it's called. It's a survival blanket thingy. Or maybe it's a space blanket. It's some kind of material that holds—"

"I know what it is," he interrupted impatiently. "Where did it come from?"

"It was in my purse." She said it casually, as if there was nothing unusual about having a high-tech piece of camping gear tucked in with the old receipts and empty gum wrappers. "Sit down and let me take a look at your shoulder."

Cole stared at her a moment longer before sinking to his knees on the blanket. It crackled slightly but it was much warmer than the ground had been. He set the first-aid kit down.

"You keep a blanket in your purse?"

"Yes." Her tone was such that she might as well have added *doesn't everyone?* "We need to get your coat and shirt off."

He must have lost more blood than he'd realized, Cole thought. Did blood loss cause hallucinations? Neatly arranged on one corner of the silvery blanket was a bottle of spring water, a small box of crackers, four cans of sardines, a Swiss Army knife big enough to hold a chain saw, a traveler's sewing kit, a handful of tea bags, envelopes of instant cocoa and a jumbled assortment of travel-size toothpastes, shampoos and deodorants.

"Did you go shopping while I was gone?" he asked.

Addie followed his eyes. She flushed and her chin seemed to come up a little. "That was in my purse, too."

"All of it?" Cole looked at the large bag with new respect. "You don't happen to have a car in there, do you?"

"Let's get your coat off," she said, ignoring the facetious question.

Cole obediently shrugged his good shoulder out of the black leather flight jacket. He allowed Addie to help him ease the other side off. From the distress in her eyes and the way she chewed on her lip, he suspected the operation caused her nearly as much pain as it caused him.

"You've lost a lot of blood," she said as the coat came away, revealing the back of his blue chambray shirt, completely soaked in blood.

"There's more where that came from," Cole said, trying to ignore the pain that radiated outward from the injury. Damned if he'd ever had a cut that hurt like this one. He brought his other hand up and began unbuttoning his shirt. To distract himself, he focused his attention on the odd assortment of items that anchored one corner of the blanket. "Do you always carry all that stuff in your purse?"

"Only when I travel." Addie's tone didn't encourage more questions but Cole couldn't restrain his curiosity.

"I've never been there, but I think South Dakota is a reasonably civilized place. They have grocery stores and maybe even restaurants."

"I'm sure they do." She pressed her lips together as she helped him ease the shirt off his right arm and then began peeling the blood-soaked fabric away from his back. "This is going to hurt," she said.

He could have told her that the warning was unnecessary. It *already* hurt. But it hurt a great deal more when she tried to pull his shirt away from the wound in his shoulder. Despite himself, Cole flinched and a muffled oath escaped from between his gritted teeth.

"I'm sorry," Addie said. He felt the anxious look she threw him.

"It's okay. Just yank it off and get it over with."

"I can't. There's something . . . stuck in the wound. Your shirt's caught on it."

That explained the pain, Cole thought. When he'd rolled them away from the plane, he'd apparently come down on something sharp enough to slice through his jacket and shirt and bury itself in his shoulder.

"What does it look like?"

"I don't know. There's so much blood." Addie's voice sounded thin and strained and Cole cursed the location of the injury that prevented him from dealing with it himself. Not even a contortionist would have been able to tend to a wound just above his own shoulder blade. If Addie couldn't handle it . . .

"Let me try and clean the area," she said, reaching for the bottled water. He was relieved to see that her hand was steady. The water felt cold against his back and it seemed to burn when it came into contact with the wound. Cole's breath hissed from between his teeth but he didn't flinch.

"Can you see it now?" he asked.

"I can see something but I can't tell what it is."

"Can you get hold of it and pull it out?"

There was a long silence. Addie sat back on her heels next to him, her eyes meeting his. She looked as pale as if she were the one who'd lost a lot of blood and her eyes stood out in huge blue pools against the pallor of her face. Cole didn't say anything. He simply looked at her. He knew she wanted to say no, wanted to tell him she couldn't do it. But he'd learned something about her in the past hour and he wasn't really surprised when she nodded.

"I can try. I'm afraid it's going to hurt." If he hadn't thought it might sound sarcastic, Cole would have pointed out that he'd figured as much.

"Pain means nothing to us macho types," he said instead, giving her a crooked grin.

It would have been nice if that had been the truth, he thought a few minutes later as Addie probed the wound in his back, trying to get a grip on whatever was embedded there. Though it couldn't have been much above sixty degrees, sweat bathed his entire body, a clammy, sick kind of sweat. Twice, she got hold of the object, only to have her fingers slip loose. Each time, it felt as if she'd just driven a knife into his shoulder. Only the knowledge that she was probably suffering almost as much as he was enabled Cole to choke back the urge to curse a blue streak.

"I've got it," she whispered, speaking to herself as much as to him.

"Pull it out," Cole said shortly.

Addie gritted her teeth together so hard that her jaw ached from the pressure. Afraid that her fingers might slip again if she tried to hurry, she moved slowly, finally pulling free a ragged splinter of metal that had been buried in the thick muscle of his shoulder.

"I've got it!" But her triumph was momentary. Blood welled up from the deep wound, running in a terrifying river down the tanned skin of Cole's back. She grabbed for a wad of gauze taken from the first-aid kit and laid ready.

"Let it bleed," Cole said. His voice was a barely audible rasp. "It will help cleanse the wound."

Addie saw the wisdom in what he was saying. A deep puncture wound like his was hard to clean thoroughly. The blood would help carry away any dirt or bits of cloth from his shirt. As long as he didn't lose too much blood, she thought uneasily.

He turned his head to look at the object she'd taken from his back. "Probably a piece of the plane. Damned thing was out to get me one way or another. Why do you carry all that stuff with you when you travel?" he asked abruptly, seeking something to distract him from the hot pain in his shoulder.

He felt the quick, uncertain glance Addie threw him. "I'm . . . I'm afraid of flying," she said, blurting the words out in a rush.

Cole stared at her blankly for a moment and then looked at the pile of goods. "You figure sardines and crackers help keep the plane in the air?"

"No. I-it's stupid, but I figured that if I was prepared for a crash, it wouldn't happen. Sort of a reverse psychology kind of thing," she finished in a mutter.

Cole looked at her and then turned his head to study the wreck of his plane. "It didn't work," he noted expressionlessly.

"I know." Addie sighed and looked at her huge purse. "I can't tell you how many planes I've dragged that thing on and off of, half believing it was the only thing that kept us in the air. I guess I could have saved myself a lot of effort."

"It wasn't a completely wasted effort," Cole said solemnly. "At least we've got something for dinner."

Their eyes met and suddenly they were both laughing.

Chapter 2

"You haven't asked what happened," Cole said, breaking the almost peaceful silence that had fallen between them.

It had been over an hour since the crash. His shoulder had been bandaged and he'd taken two aspirin, washed down with spring water. His plane—and sole source of income—was a hopeless wreck and there was no way of knowing when—or even *if*—they were going to be found, but they were alive, the sun was shining and the pain in his shoulder had subsided to a bearable ache. Life was, if not exactly good, at least considerably better than it had been an hour ago.

Addie had been contemplating the elastic bandage that wrapped her ankle. Cole's comment brought her eyes to his face. "What happened with what?"

"With the plane. You haven't asked what happened to force us down."

"You said one of the de-icers failed," she said, and lifted her shoulders in a shrug as if that was all the explanation she expected or needed.

"Don't you want to know whether or not it was my fault?"

"It doesn't seem likely," she said, looking surprised that he should even mention the possibility.

"Why isn't it likely?" Cole was intrigued by her calm assumption.

Addie frowned, her dark brows drawing together as she considered his question. "I guess it's kind of like packing your own chute," she said slowly. "Since you were going to be flying the plane, it doesn't make much sense that you'd be careless with it."

"That's true, but I suspect most people would feel better if they had someone to blame."

"It's silly to think that everything in life is somehow under our control. More things happen by sheer chance than by planning."

"I agree."

Silence fell again. It occurred to Cole that most people would have felt the need to fill the silence, to talk about what had happened, to discuss what they should do next. But Addie didn't seem to feel any such urge. She sat on the blanket, her arms wrapped around her updrawn knees, her eyes focused on the wooded slope that stretched out below them. Her expression was pensive.

"Why here?" she asked suddenly. She turned her head to look at him. "You said this mountain looked softer than the others, but it didn't seem particularly soft to me."

"It's all relative," Cole said. "There weren't as many trees. I figured I could get an easier landing here." He followed Addie's gaze to the battered remains of his plane and his mouth twisted in a rueful smile. "Yeah, well, it could have been worse."

"True."

They fell silent again. After all that had happened, there was something almost soporific about just sitting and listening to the profound stillness that drifted across the mountain. Realizing that he was on the verge of sinking into a stupor, Cole roused himself.

"It's going to be dark soon. We should start thinking about getting situated for the night."

Addie had been trying to avoid thinking that far ahead but there was no denying that the light was fading and the temperature, which hadn't been balmy to start with, was edging downward.

"I don't suppose there's much chance we're going to be found before dark?" she asked, only half kidding. She would have given a great deal to hear Cole say that he expected a rescue party to appear at any moment.

"Not tonight." There was a note of finality in his tone that made her uneasy.

"Tomorrow?"

"Could be." But he didn't sound hopeful and Addie felt her uneasiness increase. He got up with something less than his usual grace, his movements stiff with the need to favor his injured shoulder. "I think our best bet is to spend the night in the plane. It should be a little warmer than sleeping in the open.''

"Is that a good idea?'' Addie rose also, but eyed the plane uneasily. It had to be her imagination that gave the battered nose a faintly malevolent expression. "I don't want to wake up and find myself heading down the mountain.''

"It's not going to come loose from that ledge,'' Cole said without hesitation. Addie decided to take his word for it. She wasn't particularly anxious to spend the night in the open. Besides, there was another fear overriding the possibility of the plane falling the rest of the way down the mountain.

"We *are* going to be found, right? Somebody is already looking for us?'' She couldn't keep the anxiety from her tone.

Cole's first instinct was to offer a blanket reassurance. But she deserved better than that. After the way she'd held together through everything that had happened, it would be incredibly patronizing of him to start lying to her now.

"I don't know,'' he admitted. He smiled crookedly, his eyes meeting hers. "I radioed our location. If we were high enough to prevent the mountains from blocking the signal, it will still only give any rescue operations a rough idea of where we are—within twenty miles or so.''

"That's not exactly pinpoint accuracy,'' Addie said uneasily.

Traces of color had begun to creep back into her face, but they were gone now, leaving her eyes almost painfully blue against the pallor of her skin. Cole half wished he had opted to be patronizing rather than honest.

"It's not quite as bleak as it sounds," he said. "There's an emergency transmitter on the plane that sends out a signal that's picked up by satellite."

"Well, that doesn't sound too bad." Addie said, looking so relieved that Cole was glad he hadn't mentioned that the system, while good, was hardly infallible. There was nothing to be gained by anticipating all possible disasters right this second.

"I have even better news," he said, bending to pick up the silvery blanket on which they'd been sitting. "A buddy of mine owns a piece of land in Montana. Since the only time I go camping is when he and I go up there, I just leave my camping gear in the Beech Craft. There's no fuel for the camp stove or lanterns but we've got a sleeping bag and some dehydrated food. Practically the lap of luxury."

"I'm starting to feel almost pampered," Addie said dryly.

Considering everything she'd gone through during the course of the day, Addie had expected to fall asleep the minute her head hit the pillow. She might have done just that, if there had been a pillow for her head to hit. Because, if there had been a pillow, there would have been a bed and, if there had been a bed, she certainly wouldn't have been sharing it with Cole Walker. And it was his large presence only inches away that was making sleep such a distant possibility.

She lay on her side, her hands tucked under her cheek, her eyes wide open and staring into the dark-

ness, which, since Cole had pulled the plane's door
shut, was almost complete. She could, if she concentrated, just make out the outline of the door. So much
the better for sleep, she tried to tell herself—no dis-
tractions. But a strobe light flashing overhead couldn't
have been any more distracting than the feel of Cole's
large body pressed against her back.

Ignore him, her practical side ordered briskly.

Impossible, was the immediate response. It simply
wasn't possible to ignore over six feet of solid muscle
and masculinity. She hadn't been able to ignore him
when they were sitting in the cockpit together, separated by a demure three feet of air. She certainly
couldn't do it when his bare chest was only inches
away from her back and she could feel the muscled
length of his legs almost touching hers.

Undoubtedly, she should be thinking about weightier issues. A brush with death should probably make
her contemplate things like the meaning of life and the
importance of having a will drawn up. The fact that
she was lying here thinking about nothing but Cole
Walker's lean body and the wicked charm of his smile
was proof positive that she was a shallow person.

She was beyond tired. Exhaustion had crept into
every pore. Given that, she should have been able to
just close her eyes and forget all about the warm body
lying next to hers. Squeezing her eyes shut, she willed
herself to pretend that Cole wasn't there at all, that she
was alone in her own bed.

Her eyes flew open as Cole shifted position slightly.
Holding her breath, Addie tried to make herself as
small as possible. If only the air mattress he'd put be-

neath them was a little wider, she thought, feeling his leg brush against hers. It could have been worse, of course. Without the air mattress, they would have been obliged to see if two people would fit in a sleeping bag made for one. As it was, they could lie on the air mattress and spread the open sleeping bag over them as a blanket. His leg brushed hers again and she tried to squeeze closer to the edge of the air mattress.

"I won't bite," Cole said quietly into the darkness.

"I know." Addie's breath left her in a rush. "It's just that I'm not really used to sleeping with anyone. At least, not under these conditions," she added quickly, afraid she'd revealed too much about her love life, or rather, the lack thereof.

"This isn't exactly normal for me, either," Cole stated dryly. "This is one of the reasons I don't usually take passengers."

"What do you mean?"

"Well, at least, if I'm carrying freight and I crash my plane, I don't have to share my sleeping bag." His long-suffering tone made Addie give a quick involuntary smile. "Although," he continued thoughtfully, "I did once transport an extremely nervous poodle for a wealthy woman. She and her husband had divorced recently and had joint custody of the dog—alternate weeks. Everything was fine until he moved to Reno. Since she was still living in Santa Barbara, you can imagine what a problem it created."

"You're making this up," she accused him.

"No, I'm not," he protested in a tone of offended innocence. "I took Ralph from Santa Barbara to Reno and back again every week for almost four months."

"Ralph?" Addie's voice shook with laughter. "They named their poodle Ralph?"

"No. She called him Precious and the husband called him Winston. *I* called him Ralph."

She giggled. "Now I know you're making this up."

"It's God's honest truth," he insisted. "Ralph and I became pretty good friends."

"You're not still taking the poor dog back and forth, are you?"

"No. It turns out the dog had originally belonged to the wife's first husband. He'd left the dog with her while he was in Europe for a couple of years. When he moved back to the States, he insisted on reclaiming full custody of Robespierre."

"R-Robespierre?" Addie could hardly get the word out.

"Yeah. Apparently that was the name on Ralph's papers. Last I heard, he was living in Baton Rouge."

"You must miss him," she said, giggling.

"Well, he wasn't bad company. Not much of a conversationalist but he was a pretty good listener."

Cole felt the rigid tension draining from Addie's body. The light story had had the desired effect. She'd been holding herself so stiff that it was like lying next to a block of wood. And every time he so much as twitched a toe, she'd jumped as if someone had jabbed her with a cattle prod. If he'd thought it was because she was afraid of him, he might have considered being offended. But he was fairly sure that it was ner-

vous exhaustion rather than fear of him that had her
so tense.

"Do you transport much livestock?" she asked,
sounding almost relaxed.

"No. Almost all of my business is freight. Passengers—on four legs or two—are pretty rare." He shifted
into a more comfortable position and was relieved
when she didn't even seem to notice.

"Don't you do charters?"

"People who can afford to charter a plane generally want a few more luxuries than I can provide. Last
time my brother Gage flew with me, he complained
that he nearly froze to death, said his butt was numb
for days and that his ears didn't stop ringing for a
week."

"It wasn't that bad," Addie protested.

"That's what I told Gage. Actually, I accused him
of preferring sissy planes with pressurized cabins,
peanuts and flight attendants and said he had no ap-
preciation for life stripped to the basics."

"Was he suitably embarrassed?" Addie asked, and
Cole found himself wishing he could see the smile he
could hear in her voice. One thing he'd noticed was
that her smile lit up her whole face.

"He seemed to think that peanuts and flight attendants were about as basic as he wanted to get."

He frowned into the darkness. He'd been trying not
to think about his family. They were going to be worried sick when he didn't make his scheduled landing in
South Dakota.

"You have a little girl, don't you?" she asked as if
she'd read his thoughts.

"Yeah." Mary was the center of his world. "I left her with my brother Gage and his wife. They have a son who's a little younger than Mary."

"Then you know she's being taken care of."

"And probably being spoiled rotten," he said with a quick half smile. "But she's going to be scared. It's been just the two of us since she was a baby."

"What about her mother?" Addie asked tentatively.

"Roxie?" From his tone, Cole was surprised by the mention of her. "She's been gone for a long time."

"I know how hard that is. I lost my own mother when I was twelve," Addie said, her heart going out to the motherless little girl.

"Roxie's not dead," Cole said, correcting her assumption. "She just didn't want to be a mother. We were divorced before Mary was a year old."

His casual tone precluded any offer of sympathy and sparked Addie's curiosity. He didn't sound heartbroken, but surely he'd loved his ex-wife at one time. She found herself wondering what kind of woman could walk away from her child, not to mention walk away from a man like Cole Walker.

"At least Mary had her father," she said, unaware of the faint wistfulness in her voice.

"Did you lose your father at the same time as your mother?" Cole asked sympathetically.

"My father's not dead," Addie said, wondering what had made him think otherwise.

"Sorry. When you commented that at least Mary had me, I got the impression..." He ended with a verbal shrug. "Sorry."

"I didn't mean to imply that I didn't have my father at all. I guess I was just thinking that it sounds as if you and your daughter are close. Not that my father and I aren't. Close, I mean. We are. In a way." Addie stumbled to a halt, aware that she was not only babbling, she was offering explanations where none were needed.

"Does your father live in Santa Barbara?" Cole asked, wisely avoiding comment on her tangled explanation.

"Yes. But he's in Alaska right now. He's not due back until next week."

"Probably just as well. At least he won't have to worry about you."

"Oh, he wouldn't worry." Addie felt Cole's surprise and quickly corrected herself. "I mean, he *would,* of course, but he isn't the sort to pace the floor or sit by the phone."

Actually, the trick would be to get him to remember he *had* a daughter long enough for him to worry about her, she thought, and then was ashamed of herself for being so disloyal.

"Pacing doesn't accomplish much," Cole said.

"It's just that he's got so many other things on his mind," Addie said, offering him the excuse she'd given to herself so many times over the years. She was so busy making sure he understood that her father wasn't an unfeeling parent that she hardly noticed Cole easing closer to her, drawing his knees up so that her body was cradled by his, yet still separated by a scant few inches.

"Actually, you may have heard of him. Ronald Smith?"

"Doesn't ring any bells," Cole admitted.

Addie felt an odd little rush of pleasure at his blank tone. She'd spent her life living in the shadow of her father's genius. In academic circles, being Ronald Smith's daughter carried certain expectations with it—expectations she'd never felt herself capable of meeting.

"He's a paleontologist," she said. "He's made some wonderful discoveries on this continent. I've been working as his research assistant for the last few years. Most of his work has been published in academic journals but he has done some work for the more general reader. He's had articles in several magazines."

"I'm afraid my taste in books runs more to mysteries and thrillers," Cole said, his tone politely regretful. "I wouldn't think January in Alaska would be the best season for digging up bones."

"He's not on a dig. He's studying the Bering Strait and gathering information on the Bering Land Bridge. It doesn't exist anymore, of course, but that's how humans reached this continent, walking across it from Siberia." A sudden yawn caught her off guard. "Excuse me." She yawned again, aware that her eyelids were starting to feel very heavy. "My father thinks humans reached this continent much earlier than the commonly accepted dates. He's doing research for a book he's writing to support his theory."

"I have this vague idea that books written to prove controversial theories are inclined to start polite wars in academic circles," Cole said.

Addie chuckled sleepily. "Not as polite as you might think. You'd be surprised just how ugly things get when you threaten someone's favorite theory."

"Paperweights at dawn?"

"Just about." She yawned again, murmuring a slurred apology.

"That's okay. I can hardly keep my eyes open," Cole said. "It's hard to believe everything that's happened today. Maybe I should have read my horoscope this morning. It might have given me some warning."

He continued to talk, saying nothing of consequence, keeping his voice low and almost monotonic. It didn't take long for Addie's breathing to deepen and slow. Asleep, her body relaxed, settling naturally back against the support of his.

Cole let his voice trail off. Releasing his breath on an almost soundless sigh, he closed his eyes. God, he was tired. The last time he could remember being this exhausted was when Mary was a baby and suffering from colic. He'd spent uncounted hours walking the floor with her, getting to the point where just the thought of a full night's sleep was enough to make him want to cry as loudly as his infant daughter.

He opened his eyes again, staring into the darkness that wrapped the interior of the downed Beech Craft. Mary. The thought of her made his chest ache with a pain much sharper than the one in his shoulder. Sometimes she seemed so much older than her age that he'd joke about her being seven going on seventy, but she was still just a very little girl. Whenever he took a flight that was going to keep him out overnight, he called her as soon as he arrived at his destination. When he didn't call, she'd worry. The more time passed, the more she'd worry. By now it would be obvious that something was very wrong. She'd be scared and probably trying to hide it.

Stop it. Thinking about it doesn't change things. He drew a deep breath and released it slowly. Gage and Kelsey would look out for Mary. In fact, his whole family would look out for her. She might be frightened but she was far from alone.

He wasn't alone, either, Cole thought as Addie shifted in her sleep. He slid his arm around her waist and eased her back against him. She murmured something indistinguishable but didn't try to pull away. Instead she relaxed more fully, her small body fitting itself to his as if they'd been sleeping together for years. Cole adjusted his own position to hers, wishing he'd had the foresight to buy a wider air mattress. Even better, he could have brought two sleeping bags. And while he was at it, he might as well wish for a briefcase-size personal helicopter like George Jetson's, he thought ruefully. Then he could just unfold it and whisk them out of the mountains.

If he had to make a forced landing in the middle of nowhere, he wished it hadn't been on one of the rare flights where he was carrying a passenger. He didn't like the additional responsibility that Addie represented. And, although he was too tired to worry about it tonight, he wasn't particularly looking forward to spending another night with her snuggled so confidingly against him. When he was less achy and tired, her curvy little body could prove quite a distraction.

He yawned and let his eyes drift shut. Maybe they'd get lucky and someone would find them tomorrow.

The Family

The shrill jangle of the telephone startled Keefe Walker out of a deep sleep. Rolling over in bed, he stretched out one long arm and dragged the receiver off the base.

"'Lo." His greeting was mumbled and less than friendly. If this was a wrong number, he was going to reach right through the line and strangle whoever was on the other end. He'd been up all night last night, tending to a mare who was having trouble giving birth to her first foal. After getting less than three hours' sleep in the past thirty-six, he did not appreciate having his sleep interrupted.

"Keefe? It's Gage."

Keefe's irritation vanished and his eyes snapped open. His brother wouldn't be calling at midnight without good reason. "Has Kelsey gone into labor early?"

Kelsey was Gage's wife and they were expecting a baby in a little less than a month.

"No. It's not Kelsey." Gage hesitated a moment. "It's Cole."

"What about him?" Keefe dragged himself upright in bed, his heart beating much too quickly, his exhaustion forgotten.

"He was flying a friend of Nikki's to South Dakota today—yesterday," Gage corrected himself. "He never made it there."

"What do you know?"

"Not much. Some little airport in Wyoming picked up part of a Mayday. They've got a rough location. If he was in the mountains, the signal may have gotten chopped up." He didn't need to add that if Cole had been in the mountains, he would have had a hell of a time finding a place to bring the plane down safely.

"What's being done?" Keefe rolled out of bed and tucked the receiver between his chin and his shoulder as he reached for the jeans he'd tossed over a chair when he came to bed.

"Not much until morning. He's... There's an emergency transmitter on the plane, but if he went down in the Rockies..." Gage didn't complete the sentence but Keefe knew what he meant. The peaks could cause problems with any radio signal.

"Where's Mary?" He dragged the jeans up over his lean hips and reached for a shirt.

"She's with us. Kelsey just got her to sleep a little while ago."

"How's she holding up?"

"You know Mary." Gage's laugh was thin. "She's trying to pretend she's not worried but she's scared to death. Hell, *I'm* scared."

"Yeah, I know." Keefe shoved his shirttail roughly into his jeans and picked up his wallet and keys from the top of the dresser. "Have you called Sam?"

"He and Nikki are on their way up from L.A. Mom was spending the weekend at their place so she's coming with them." He hesitated. "We didn't call sooner because we didn't want to push any panic buttons if we didn't have to. And Kelsey thought it would only scare Mary more if the whole family suddenly showed up."

"She's smart enough to know there's something wrong by now."

Gage sighed. "Yeah. She knows. We had a hell of a time getting her to sleep. It doesn't help that she knows Danny's father is dead." Danny was Gage's five-year-old stepson. "It makes losing a parent seem all too possible."

"Seems to me Mary already knows it's possible to lose a parent," Keefe said. He sat down on the edge of the bed and yanked on a pair of socks.

"Yeah, but she knows her mother isn't dead. Roxie may not be in the picture but she's still out there somewhere."

"So is Cole," Keefe said shortly. He snagged his boots from where they lay at the foot of the bed.

"Yeah."

"I've got to wake Jace and tell him what's going on and then I'll be on my way."

"We'll be here." Gage didn't argue with Keefe's decision to make the long drive to Santa Barbara. He knew that Keefe and his partner, Jace Reno, ran The Flying Ace together and that, when one of them was gone, it threw the full burden on the other's shoulders. Jace was going to have his hands more than full. But when one of the Walkers was in trouble, they all pulled together until the problem was resolved.

Gage was just hanging up the phone when Kelsey walked into the kitchen. Or, as she insisted, waddled into the kitchen. Not even under torture would Gage have admitted out loud that the description held any accuracy, but privately he had to agree that "waddle" was a pretty apt word. Nearly eight and a half months into her pregnancy, Kelsey was no longer moving either quickly or easily.

"How are the kids?" he asked.

"They're both asleep but I don't know how long they'll stay that way." Her gray eyes were dark with worry. "This makes Danny think about Rick dying and Mary thinks about Danny's father being dead and they're both scared to death." She bit her lip and looked up at him. "I don't know what to tell them."

"Come here." Gage wrapped his arms around her and pulled her close. Kelsey gave a slightly watery chuckle as he tried to maneuver around her stomach.

"I'm fat as a house."

"No bigger than a small cottage," he told her lovingly.

"Beast." She poked him in the ribs but leaned gratefully against his strength.

"Keefe is on his way," Gage said.

"That's a long drive to be starting at this hour of the night."

"He'll be okay. And he wouldn't be comfortable staying on the ranch, waiting for news. Sam and Nikki and Mom will be here in a couple of hours."

"I should make some coffee and sandwiches," Kelsey murmured.

"You should try and get a little sleep," Gage corrected her. He ran his fingers through her hair, stroking the pale blond strands back from her forehead. "I'll wake you when everyone gets here."

"The Walkers pull together," Kelsey murmured.

"Always," Gage said.

Chapter 3

The first thing Addie was aware of was that something was not right. She was lying on her side, and the pillow under her head felt as if it was full of rocks. The mattress didn't feel much better. Her face felt cold, but her body was much too warm. It felt like someone had tucked a furnace into the bed with her. Frowning, eyes still closed, she tried to brush aside the blanket only to find that something heavy lay across her waist, pinning her arm to her side.

Her eyes flew open, a quick rush of fear jolting her awake. As soon as she saw the bare interior of the plane's cabin, memories washed over her. The flight from Santa Barbara that had started out in sunshine and ended in such total disaster. No, not *total* disaster, she corrected herself. They'd survived in reasonably good shape, which kept it at least a notch above total.

A soft grumble sounded in her ear—a soft *masculine* grumble. Cole. Addie's eyes widened as she realized that the wall of heat at her back was Cole's large body. Without moving her head, she slanted a look downward at the long arm that lay outside the sleeping bag. His hand was splayed across her stomach. There was something distinctly erotic about the sight of those long fingers pressed against her. She was shocked by the thought, even more shocked to find herself wondering what it would feel like to have him hold her like that without the thickness of blanket and clothes between them.

She closed her eyes a moment, feeling her cheeks flood with color. Maybe she'd sustained a concussion in the crash. Otherwise, how could she explain the direction her thoughts had taken? Not that Cole Walker wasn't the sort of man to inspire erotic fantasies. Any woman who could see the way his eyes seemed to smile even before his mouth curved and *not* indulge in a fantasy or two was simply not human. Not to mention the shaggy blond hair that seemed to invite a woman's fingers to push it into even greater disorder. And then there was the rangy strength of his body and—

With some difficulty, Addie reined in her thoughts. That was all beside the point. She didn't have to catalog his attractions. She firmed her mouth into a prim line. It was enough to admit that Cole Walker was, quite possibly, the most devastatingly attractive man she'd ever met. But, given the circumstances, it was

hardly appropriate to be so aware of that fact. She
should have other things on her mind. Like how to get
out of their makeshift bed without waking him. Not
an easy thing to do when she'd apparently spent the
night cuddled up against him as cozily as if she slept
this way every night of her life. She did not want Cole
to wake up and find her snuggled so confidingly in his
arms.

She wasn't worried about him getting the wrong
idea. She wasn't the kind of woman about whom men
got wrong ideas. Short, slightly plump brunettes rarely
drove men wild with desire. Waking with her in his
arms wasn't likely to drive Cole into a fit of unbridled
lust, she thought with a touch of wistful regret. But
he'd probably find it as embarrassing as she did if he
realized how comfortable they'd become. Maybe she
could ease her way off the air mattress and be gone
before he woke.

But as soon as she moved, Cole stirred, his hand
flattening against her stomach and dragging her back
against his body. For a heart-stopping moment she
could feel every solid muscle of his chest pressed
against her back and the quick leap of her pulse had
nothing to do with fear or embarrassment and everything to do with plain old awareness. She sucked in a
quick, startled breath and found herself instantly released.

"Sorry." Cole's voice was low, raspy with sleep, his
breath stirring the curls over her ear.

"'S'okay." Addie spoke so quickly that her words
slurred together into one indecipherable mumble. Her
heart thudding with something approaching panic, she

scrambled to her feet. But, in her rush to put distance between them, she'd forgotten her injured ankle. The moment her weight came down on it, pain shot up her leg and the joint buckled. She tumbled backward.

Alerted by her startled cry, Cole sat up, his hands coming up automatically to catch her and break her fall. She dropped into his arms like a dead weight. A short, pungent oath escaped him as he took her weight, closing his eyes against the pain that ripped through his shoulder.

There was a moment of dead silence. He opened his eyes to see Addie staring up at him, her pretty blue eyes surprised, as if she wasn't quite sure how she'd come to be lying in his arms. As he watched, color began to run up under her fair skin, and her eyes took on a stricken look.

"Your shoulder?" she whispered, as if speaking out loud might cause him pain.

"I'll live. Your ankle?" He arched one brow in question and she nodded guiltily.

"I forgot about it. I'm sorry."

"I'm okay," he said, and hoped he wasn't lying. The sharp pain had given way to a bruised ache. "You seemed to be in something of a hurry."

"I didn't mean...I was just..." Addie's voice trailed off.

"I don't think I've ever had a woman in *that* much of a hurry to get out of bed after spending the night with me," Cole said thoughtfully.

"I wasn't.... Not you... I'm just not..." She couldn't seem to get out a complete sentence and her face was so red, it looked as if she was suffering from a fatal fever. She abruptly realized that he was still holding her. Scrambling off his lap, she knelt on the air mattress and stared at him, her eyes so full of distress that he felt guilty for teasing her.

"I'm kidding," he assured her.

"I'm just not used to waking up in bed with someone," she blurted, and then blushed even darker, as if she'd just admitted something embarrassing.

"To tell the truth, neither am I," Cole said. He saw her eyes widen a little and wondered if she'd envisioned him living the life of a swinging bachelor, with women spilling out of his bed like grapes out of a fruit bowl. Even if he'd been so inclined, common sense would have intruded. Besides, the truth was, between running a business and raising a child, he didn't have time to do any swinging.

He saw the tension ease from her and she gave him an appealingly sheepish smile. "Did I hurt your shoulder when I fell on you?"

"Didn't I already tell you that we macho types take no notice of pain?"

"I think you mentioned it yesterday." Her smile took on a mischievous edge. "So I guess that groan I heard had nothing to do with the fact that I'd just dropped on you like a ton of bricks?"

"I hardly noticed," he assured her with exaggerated indifference.

"And if I believed that, you could see about selling me some oceanfront property in Arizona."

"How did you know?" he asked, raising his brows in mock surprise.

Addie laughed, her earlier discomfort forgotten. She must have been out of her mind to even think of anything sexual in connection with herself and Cole. He probably thought of her as a fellow victim rather than as a woman.

Seeing her smile, it struck Cole that she had the most deliciously kissable mouth he'd ever seen.

Cole cupped his hands around the cup of instant cocoa, letting the heat seep into his palms. They'd set up temporary residence a few yards away from the plane. Cole had been prepared to dredge up nearly forgotten Boy Scout skills and build a fire but Addie had proven to be more than up to the challenge. With a minimum of fuss and a match drawn from the cavernous depths of her purse, she'd put together a neat little campfire.

"I'm glad I didn't have to spend the morning rubbing sticks together," Cole said.

"Matches make it a lot easier," she said with that shy smile that seemed to light her face from within.

Cole had provided a pan from his camping gear, Addie had supplied the cocoa packet and the water, and they had breakfast.

"We need to find a source of water," Cole said, frowning down into his cup. "I think I saw something that might have been a stream not too far west of here while we were still in the air. We've got plenty of fuel but we should take an inventory of the food and try to figure out how far it will stretch."

"You sound like you expect us to be here for a long time," Addie said slowly.

"I don't know how long we're going to be here." He lifted his head, his eyes meeting hers.

She was seated on a rock across the fire from him, her hair tumbling around her face in a mass of soft brown curls, her blue eyes wide with worry. Bruises left purple smudge marks on one cheekbone and the surprisingly firm thrust of her chin. Her khaki slacks were creased and dirty. He knew the matching shirt was in much the same condition though it was covered now by a thick, down jacket that seemed to swallow her small frame. There was something almost waiflike about her. Cole would have given a great deal to be able to reassure her that rescue lay just around the corner.

"They are looking for us, aren't they?"

"They're looking for us, but there's no way to know how long it's going to take for them to find us. We should do what we can to stretch our supplies, just to be safe."

"Okay." Addie nodded her agreement with that logic.

"We're lucky the weather is good," Cole said, glancing at the pale blue winter sky. "This time of year, this high up, we could have been dealing with blizzards."

After Cole left to see if he could find the stream he thought he'd seen from the air, Addie spent some time trying to feel grateful for the weather. When that palled, she tried to admire the natural beauty of her surroundings. But all she could really see was a lot of pine trees and a bunch of rocks. The most interesting thing in sight was the path the plane's landing had gouged in the earth. From there, her attention was drawn to the plane itself and she found something for which she could be truly grateful—they were alive.

When Cole returned, he found Addie still perched on the rock but she now had a steno pad balanced on her knee and was writing in it with a ballpoint.

"If you're planning on putting a note in a bottle, I've got to warn you that the tide only reaches this far inland every few million years."

Addie looked up, her mouth curving in a quick smile. "But if California finally breaks off and falls into the Pacific, we might see a wave way ahead of schedule."

"You anticipate that happening?"

"No. But it never hurts to be prepared."

He grinned. "First you shame me by building a fire faster than I can and now you're telling me to be prepared. Are you sure you didn't infiltrate a Boy Scout troop sometime during your misspent youth?"

Addie laughed softly, her eyes crinkling at the corners. "I think that's a very sexist remark. Girl Scouts learn those kinds of things, too, you know."

"How politically incorrect of me," Cole said. "I wish I'd known that when I was a kid. Maybe I could have tried infiltrating them instead of joining the Boy Scouts." He caught her doubtful look and grinned. "Hey, it worked for Dustin Hoffman in *Tootsie.*"

"I just don't see you as a Girl Scout," Addie said. Privately, she couldn't imagine any female of any age not immediately recognizing the essential masculinity of him.

"Are you suggesting I wouldn't look good in a skirt?" Cole asked, looking vaguely offended.

"The mind boggles."

"I don't know. I thought broad shoulders were an advantage for a woman."

"Not as broad as yours," she said flatly.

"Damn. I guess that means I'll have to give up my ambition to become a fashion model."

The idea of him strutting down a catwalk was enough to make Addie's eyes widen. "Not as long as the current affection for waifs prevails," she said, keeping her face straight.

Cole heaved a sigh. "The fashion world is so cruel," he said, pulling his face into a creditable expression of regret.

Addie giggled helplessly. She'd never known anyone who could make her laugh as easily as he did. She tried to imagine her father under the same circumstances, tried to picture him making jokes. But since he wasn't exactly a laugh riot under the best of conditions, it wasn't likely that a plane crash would suddenly bring out a latent sense of humor.

"If you're through dashing my dreams of a career in the world of high fashion, you might be interested in knowing that I found a stream." He set a filled water bottle down and then crouched next to the fire, stretching his hands out to the warmth. "At least we have plenty of drinking water."

"Didn't I read somewhere that you shouldn't drink water even from high in the mountains because of some kind of parasites or something?" Addie asked, eyeing the bottle uneasily.

"We'll boil it before we use it." He rubbed one hand over his face and Addie was suddenly aware of the tired lines etched around his eyes and mouth.

"How does your shoulder feel?"

"Like somebody stuck a big piece of metal in it," he said, giving her a crooked smile.

"Maybe I should take a look at it?" she suggested tentatively. He'd dismissed the same offer earlier in the day so she was hardly surprised when his response remained the same.

"It's not bothering me." He caught her doubtful look and amended the statement. "It's not bothering me any more than I'd expect it to. If you weren't planning on putting a note in a bottle, what were you writing?"

Addie accepted his obvious desire to change the subject, but she would have felt better if he'd let her look at his injury. "I was writing up an inventory of our food supplies."

Looking at the list she'd made, they tried to estimate how far their food supplies might stretch. They thought they might have enough for ten days or so.

"I hope we don't have to find out,"Addie said.

"I hope so, too."

"What if we built a signal fire, something that would put out a lot of smoke? Wouldn't that make it easier for a plane to spot us?"

"I don't know." Cole frowned, his eyes scanning the surrounding area. "We've got plenty of fuel. We could put together a pretty good size fire, but all it would take is a spark in the wrong place and we could find ourselves sitting in the middle of a forest fire.''

''I thought forest fires happened when the weather was hot.''

''They're more likely to start then, whether from natural causes or unnatural tourists, but I don't see any reason why trees wouldn't burn now. There isn't much snow on the ground. It's dry. What's to stop them from burning?'' He lifted his good shoulder in a half shrug. ''Hell, I'm no forest ranger. For all I know, there's some immutable law of nature that forests never burn in January, but I'm not sure I want to take a chance on it.''

Addie had to agree. She didn't know what the risks were, either. And their situation was bad enough without adding a forest fire to it. With a sigh, she abandoned the idea of a signal fire.

Lunch was a can of sardines from her purse and a handful of extremely stale crackers from the food that had been in the plane, washed down with water made flat and tasteless by a thorough boiling.

''Not exactly what I'd call an exquisite repast,'' Cole said as he swallowed the last cracker.

''I don't think a restaurant offering sardines and stale crackers is likely to make a big splash,'' Addie agreed. ''I have a couple of candy bars in my purse if you want dessert.''

''Let's save them for later.'' Cole shifted his shoulder gingerly, trying to ease the throbbing ache that gripped it. Catching Addie's worried look, he smiled and shook his head. ''I didn't say it didn't hurt.''

"Are you sure—"

"I'm sure," he said firmly. Even when he was a child, he hadn't liked having anyone fuss over him. When he thought about it, which wasn't often, he assumed it came from being the youngest of four boys. While there hadn't been anything he could do about his birth order, he'd been determined never to be the "baby" in the family.

"I don't suppose you have a TV in that purse of yours," he said. He leaned forward to feed a couple of sticks into the fire. "Since we have nothing better to do, maybe we could catch up on the soaps."

"I have a deck of cards," Addie said.

Cole chuckled. "Is there anything you *don't* have in that purse?"

"A television," she pointed out.

Looking at her as she dug into the cavernous depths of her purse, it occurred to Cole that, if it hadn't been for the crash, he would never have noticed what a sweet smile she had or seen the mischief that could lurk behind the soft blue of her eyes.

"Cards," she announced triumphantly, holding a slightly battered pack aloft.

"Life doesn't get any better than this," Cole said, grinning.

"Make that almost two million dollars you owe me," Cole said as he scooped up his winnings, which consisted of a handful of twigs.

"I'm starting to feel lucky, though," Addie said, her chin setting with determination.

"You said that before the last hand," he quipped.

"Yes, but this time I had a pair of eights. All I needed was one more to have three of a kind and that would have beat your two jacks because three of a kind beats two of a kind even if the two are a higher denomination, right?"

"Right." Cole held back a smile and concentrated on shuffling the cards.

He'd never played cards with anyone who had less of a poker face. When her hand was good, her eyes sparkled with pleasure. When it was bad, she frowned and her teeth worried her lower lip as if the fate of the world depended on her getting the right card. Even his seven-year-old daughter revealed less of what she was thinking when they played Go Fish.

"Maybe we should change games," he suggested.

"No. I think I'm starting to get the hang of this."

"It's just that, the way things have been going, you're losing about a million an hour to me. I'd hate to see you get in over your head," he said, tongue firmly in cheek.

"I always pay my gambling debts," Addie said, looking down her small nose at him.

"Looks to me like you're running out of sticks." Cole nodded to the pile in front of her as he dealt the cards.

"There are always more where those came from," she said, waving one hand in casual dismissal of his concern. "Your concern is appreciated but unnecessary." She set a twig in the middle of the blanket. "I'll open for one hundred thousand."

For all he knew, she actually could afford to lose a couple million, Cole thought as he matched her bet and raised her another hundred grand. Seeing her sitting cross-legged on the blanket, her hair tousled, her face bruised and her clothes dirty, it was easy to forget that she came from a very different background than his own. For some reason, the thought made him uncomfortable.

By the time the light began to fade, Addie owed Cole almost ten million dollars, but she remained optimistic that, given time, she could recoup her losses. Since she continued to telegraph her every hand, Cole thought this unlikely and advised her to avoid Las Vegas. Scooping his pile of twigs up in both hands, he tossed it onto the fire.

"Ten million bucks, up in smoke. But there's more where that came from," he said, shooting her a wicked grin.

"I wouldn't count on winning so easily tomorrow," Addie told him with a touch of offended dignity. "I'm not a beginner anymore, you know."

"I'll keep that in mind." He stood and stretched gingerly, trying to ease the kinks from his back without pulling at his injured shoulder. "What epicurean delight shall we have for dinner?"

Corned beef hash was the dish of choice. Cole made Addie laugh with his exaggerated descriptions of the culinary pleasures awaiting them as he warmed the food over the fire. Eating the slightly scorched hash, it occurred to her that she'd laughed more in the past two days than she had in the past two months. It seemed an odd sort of addendum to a plane crash.

The Family

Keefe hung up the phone and turned to look at his family. They had gathered in Kelsey's big kitchen. Sam leaned against the counter, one hand wrapped around a coffee cup, the other settled on the curve of his wife's waist. Nikki leaned into his hold, her pale gold hair contrasting with the dark fabric of Sam's shirt. Kelsey sat at the table, her chair pushed back to accommodate the heavy swell of her stomach. Gage stood behind her, his hands resting on her shoulders.

Rachel Walker sat at the table, her expression uncharacteristically still, her dark eyes empty and lost. It had been twenty years since Keefe had seen that particular expression, but he hadn't forgotten it. It was the look of a woman facing the loss of a child. Twenty years ago it had been her four-year-old daughter who had been taken from her. Now it was her youngest son.

But this was different, Keefe promised himself. Shannon might have been taken from them forever, but Cole was coming back. He refused to believe anything else.

"Kel is setting things in motion," he said, breaking the deep silence that had fallen over the room. "He's got a pilot ready to take a chopper up first thing in the morning."

"I thought search and rescue already sent a chopper up," Sam said.

"They did, but it can't hurt to have another one looking."

"Why haven't they picked up a signal from the emergency transmitter?" Gage asked the question without expectation of an answer. No one knew the answer.

Keefe shrugged and moved over to the table to pick up his cup. He was vaguely aware that the coffee had grown unpleasantly tepid but it didn't matter.

"Dead batteries, maybe," Sam suggested in response to Gage's impatient question.

"Cole wouldn't be careless about something like that," Rachel said quietly. "Not since he's had Mary."

"No. He's become more careful since he's had Mary," Keefe agreed, thinking of how reckless his youngest brother had been in the days before he'd become a father. "I'd better get going. Bill Davis said he'd meet me at the airport."

"You'll call us when you get to your friend's ranch?" Rachel looked up at her second son. "Just so we know you got there safely."

"I'll call." Keefe bent to brush a kiss across his mother's forehead, thinking that she seemed suddenly almost frail. "Do you think Mary's asleep?" he asked Kelsey as he straightened.

"I don't know." She shrugged. "She went to bed without an argument but I had the distinct impression that she was only doing it to humor me." Kelsey reached up to grip one of Gage's hands in her own. When she looked at her brother-in-law, her gray eyes were bright with tears. "She's trying so hard to pretend that she's not scared, but I know she's terrified."

"I'll look in on her before I go." As he walked down the hallway that led to the bedrooms, Keefe admitted to a cowardly hope that he'd find his niece sound asleep. But his luck was out.

The door to the guest room had been left open a crack. As soon as he pushed it open, Mary sat up in bed.

"Did you hear anything about Daddy?" In the soft golden glow of the night-light Kelsey had left burning, Mary's expression was anxious.

"Not yet, honey." Keefe crossed the room and sat down on the edge of the bed. "I just wanted to say goodbye. Bill Davis is flying me to Wyoming. A friend of mine has a ranch not too far from where they think your dad's plane went down. I figured one of us ought to be close by."

"Can I go with you?" she asked, but her eyes told him she already knew the answer.

"I think you'd better stay here," Keefe said.

"I wouldn't get in the way," she promised, breaking his heart a little.

"I know you wouldn't, but I'd be worried about you and I want to be able to concentrate on finding your dad."

She looked as if she might argue but then nodded slowly. "Okay." Her head bent, she plucked restlessly at the blanket that covered her knees. "Are you going to find Daddy?" she asked without looking up.

"I'm going to try." He would have given a great deal to be able to give her a more definite answer but he wasn't going to lie to her. Sensing that she had more to say, Keefe waited.

"Do you think…" She stopped and swallowed hard before lifting her eyes to his face. In their chocolate brown depths, he saw the fear she was trying so hard to hide. "Do you think he's dead?" she whispered.

"No, I don't." The answer came straight from his heart. There was no logic behind it, no fact to support it, nothing but the gut level feeling that Cole wasn't—couldn't be—dead.

"Me, neither." Mary drew a shuddering breath, her fragile shoulders straightening subtly, as if a weight had been lifted from them. Keefe offered up a prayer that the reassurance he'd given her hadn't been misguided.

Chapter 4

The second day after the crash, Cole woke feeling as warm as if he'd been sleeping under a desert sun and with a headache thrumming behind his eyes.

Forcing his eyelids up, he stared at the interior of what remained of his plane and considered his symptoms. The headache could be caused by any one of a dozen sources, starting with the fact that his folded jacket made a lumpy and uncomfortable pillow. Feeling too warm was also easily explained. It had been a long time since he'd had a fever but there was no mistaking the dry heat that enveloped his body.

Just what he needed. Cole closed his eyes. From the way his shoulder was throbbing, there was no doubt about the source of the fever. The wound was infected. He should have let Addie take a look at it yesterday when she'd wanted to. Now he was probably going to get gangrene and his arm was going to fall off. And the way his luck had been running lately, his headache was probably just the initial symptom of a fatal brain tumor.

Nothing like falling headlong into a vat of self-pity, Walker.

His mouth curving in a wry smile, he opened his eyes again. Addie was still asleep, her small body curled confidingly against his. Cole's arm rested over her, his fingers splayed across her stomach. Under other circumstances, the casual intimacy of their sleeping arrangements might have inspired some lascivious thoughts, he thought idly. Addie mumbled something unintelligible in her sleep and shifted position slightly, tucking her bottom more firmly into the curve of his thighs in the process.

Cole drew a slow, shallow breath. Come to think of it, maybe lascivious thoughts weren't out of the question, even under the current circumstances. Not even a headache and a fever were enough to make him completely unaware of the curvy little body pressed so firmly against his. Despite the current fashion for women to have lean, muscular bodies, Cole thought there was a great deal to be said for a woman who was all soft curves and warmth.

Cool it, Walker. This isn't the time or the place. Only a total jerk would put the moves on a woman in a situation like this.

Of course, there is always the chance that she wouldn't mind *if you put the moves on her,* a small voice whispered.

Yeah, and maybe fever has fried your brain.

Disgusted with himself for feeling tempted, even momentarily, Cole rolled out of bed. He picked up his boots and his coat and padded, stocking-footed, across the plane's tilted floor. There was no way to open the door quietly but he was more concerned with putting some distance between himself and his companion than he was with leaving her sleep undisturbed.

The cold mountain air slapped him in the face as soon as he stepped outside. It couldn't have been any warmer inside the plane but there was something about the thin morning sunlight that made the cold seem sharper outside. Cole glanced at the sky but it looked the same as it had for the past two days—a pale blue arc stretched from one peak to another. No clouds, which was good, and no sign of search planes, which wasn't so good.

Lowering his head, Cole shrugged into his coat, biting off a curse when the movement pulled at the wound in his shoulder. Two days and he hadn't so much as *heard* a search plane going over. Had they been too low when the Mayday went out? But even if the mountains had blocked the radio signal, what about the EMT? The signal it transmitted should have been picked up by satellite. Were the mountains somehow blocking that signal, too? And if that was the case, what the hell was he supposed to do about it?

Addie opened her eyes in time to see Cole silhouetted in the doorway for an instant before he moved out of sight. Still half-asleep and not terribly anxious to leave the relative warmth of the sleeping bag, she turned over, tugged its bulky softness closer around her and tried to go back to sleep.

But without Cole's large presence, the makeshift bed seemed empty and the cold air seemed to creep under the sleeping bag, no matter how tightly she wrapped it around herself. She could get used to sleeping with him, she thought groggily. And she couldn't say she'd mind if they did more than simply sleep together.

Good Lord, where had that thought come from? Addie's eyes flew open, sleep forgotten. She'd known the man for barely two days. She couldn't honestly be thinking that she'd like to... to sleep with him. Could she?

In a New York minute!

Her face went hot at the shameless promptness with which she answered her own question. She sat up, oblivious to the cold air rushing over her as the sleeping bag slid to her waist. Pressing her fingers to her flushed cheeks, Addie stared blankly at the curved wall of the plane. What on earth had happened to her? She didn't normally think about going to bed with a man two days after she met him. Actually, she didn't normally think about going to bed with any man, no matter how long she'd known him. She was about as far from promiscuous as it was possible to get without still being pure as the driven snow.

Yes, but Cole Walker isn't just any *man,* a shameless voice whispered. *He's gorgeous.*

But she was past the age where good looks alone were enough to inspire lust.

Don't kid yourself, the wicked voice insisted. *A man who looks like that would inspire lust even if you had one foot in the grave.*

Feeling the color in her cheeks deepen, Addie wished she could attribute the painfully blunt thoughts to concussion or perhaps an alternate personality brought to life by the stress of the crash. Unfortunately, neither explanation seemed plausible.

She hadn't attained the ripe old age of twenty-seven without meeting other men who attracted her. Nor had she lived like a nun. Although not far from it. She'd dabbled her toes in the waters of sexual freedom. In her junior year in college, there had been a fellow student at UC Santa Barbara. He'd been a philosophy major and their courtship—if it could be labeled such—had consisted of deeply meaningful talks held over endless cups of herbal tea.

She had thought she might be in love with him and when he'd nudged her in the direction of sleeping with him, she hadn't resisted. Afterward she'd realized that she'd been driven as much by curiosity as by any attraction she felt for him. A few hurried and thoroughly unsatisfying gropings on his futon had made her regret the curiosity and served to put a heavy damper on the attraction. She'd felt nothing but relief when Duane hadn't expressed any burning desire to continue the relationship. Her first—and last—love affair had ended with a fizzle rather than a bang. And she hadn't been in any hurry to repeat the experience.

She was smart enough to realize that her brief experience was not the last word on sex. There had to be more to it or the human race would be in serious danger of extinction. She was not averse to trying it again, but opportunity and desire hadn't coincided. While she wasn't a raving beauty, neither was she unattractive. There had been men who'd expressed interest in her. She'd dated a little since Duane, but it had never gone further than that.

Now, here she was, thinking wistfully about going to bed with a man she barely knew. Throwing back the sleeping bag, she reached for her shoes, giving herself a mild scold as she pulled them on. Considering the circumstances, she should have more important things on her mind than Cole Walker's undeniable attractions. There was the matter of survival, for example.

When she limped out of the plane a few minutes later, Addie felt self-conscious, half-afraid that Cole would only have to look at her to know what she'd been thinking. If he were to guess anything of what had gone through her head, she'd have to find a cliff and jump off it, she promised herself.

He'd started a fire and was crouched beside it, staring into the flames as if mesmerized. Acutely aware of the recent turn of her thoughts, Addie hesitated a moment, staring at his broad back, her teeth worrying her lower lip. But she couldn't exactly avoid him. It was silly to even think about it. Yesterday, she'd thought that he was more comfortable to be with than any other man she'd ever known. Nothing had changed except that she'd become aware that her attraction to him ran deeper than she'd realized. Taking a deep breath, she moved forward.

"Good morning."

She saw Cole start at the sound of her voice, as if he'd been so absorbed in his thoughts that he hadn't heard her approach. He rose and turned to face her. Something in his expression made her pause. He looked older—harder, somehow—than he had the day before. A two-day growth of beard shadowed his jaw and his dark gold hair tumbled onto his forehead in heavy waves, making him look slightly unkempt and just a little dangerous. Addie was beyond feeling surprised when her stomach clenched in helpless visceral response to his masculinity.

"I brought coffee," she said, forcing her thoughts into more mundane channels. She held up the jar of instant that had been in his supplies. "It's not exactly fresh ground but it's better than nothing."

"It's probably stale," Cole said.

"Probably. Since I think all coffee tastes pretty rancid, I'm not likely to notice the difference," she said cheerfully.

"Lucky for you," Cole said with a half smile that didn't quite reach his eyes. He took the jar from her and knelt to pour water into their single pan before balancing it carefully on rocks set in the center of the fire ring. When the task was done, he stayed where he was, staring at the battered pan as if it held the secret to eternal life.

Addie sank down on the flat rock that had become her favorite perch, feeling an uneasiness that had nothing to do with her newly acknowledged awareness of him. Something was obviously bothering him.

"I think there's a law of physics that states that a watched pot never boils," she said when the silence threatened to become uncomfortable.

Cole looked up, a quick smile flickering across his face. "I've heard that, but I figured it was an old wives' tale."

Addie shook her head, her expression serious. "There was a study done at MIT a few years ago that proved it beyond a shadow of a doubt. I seem to recall that researchers linked it to Einstein's theory of relativity—something about time warping when you watch a pot."

"I can't quite picture a bunch of scientists, clipboards poised, standing around staring at pots of water, waiting for them to boil." This time the smile reached his eyes, driving out the shadows for a moment.

"No sacrifice is too extreme in the pursuit of scientific enlightenment," Addie intoned solemnly, and was rewarded by his appreciative grin. But it faded too quickly, the grim lines digging in around his mouth and eyes again.

Addie felt her stomach clench with sudden nerves. Something was wrong but she couldn't bring herself to come right out and ask him. Despite the enforced intimacy of the past couple of days, she didn't know him well. Just because they'd survived a forced landing together didn't mean he had to share his every thought with her.

Maybe she was reading too much into his mood, she told herself. Nothing infuriated her father more than to be badgered with questions when he fell into an abstracted silence, which he did frequently. The best thing to do was to just act as if everything was normal. Always assuming you could apply the word "normal" to their situation.

"Last night, I dreamed that we were rescued," she said, keeping her tone deliberately light and unconcerned. "A huge jetliner set down right over there and a flight attendant took our tickets. I don't know where we got the tickets, but in the dream it seemed perfectly logical that we had them. And I didn't question how the plane managed to land, either. Charlton Heston was the pilot." Her forehead creased in a frown. "I don't know why Charlton Heston, unless it's because he always looks so solid and dependable. I mean, how could you not feel good about having Moses as your pilot?"

"They're not coming," Cole said. He stood, but stared down at the fire rather than look at her.

"I wasn't really expecting Moses. Or Charlton Heston, for that matter, but somebody's bound to—"

"There's nobody coming." His tone was so flat and emotionless that Addie thought she must have misunderstood him.

"What?"

"The EMT isn't working." He jammed his hands into the pockets of his jacket.

"What's an EMT?" she asked, bewildered and starting to feel a little scared.

"The transmitter I told you about. The one that's supposed to be sending out a signal that will be picked up by satellite and lead search and rescue people to our location. It's not sending out a damned thing." He shot the information at her, his voice clipped and hard.

"Why not?" Somewhere inside, Addie could feel panic start to churn, but she subdued it ruthlessly.

"The battery leaked and the whole freaking box is full of corrosion."

She didn't say anything for a moment, digesting this and what it meant to them. She didn't like the conclusions she came to. If there was no signal... Swallowing hard, she stifled the panic that fluttered in the pit of her stomach. Giving in to fear wasn't going to accomplish anything.

"I don't suppose you have another battery handy?" she asked finally, her mouth curving in a slightly shaky smile.

"Hell no! I put this one in less than a year ago. And even if I did have another one, the inside of the box is full of battery acid. God knows what kind of damage it's done. I'd need a box of baking soda just to clean it up so I could see if there's anything left."

"Maybe I should add baking soda to my list of travel supplies," Addie said, staring down into the fire.

Cole stared at her in disbelief. She sounded as calm as if he'd just told her that he thought it might rain. Didn't she understand what he was telling her?

"If we had a truckload of baking soda, it wouldn't do us any good because I don't have another battery. Not to mention any parts I might need."

"That's true." She paused, her expression so still that he couldn't even guess what she was thinking. "I think the water's about ready." She reached for one of the tin cups she'd brought from the plane.

"No one is looking for us," Cole said, speaking slowly and distinctly so there could be no mistaking his meaning. He was almost relieved to see that Addie's hand was not quite steady. It was the first indication he'd seen that she understood what he was trying to tell her.

"You said you'd radioed our position before we...before we landed." She had to stop and swallow before she could finish the sentence.

"That only provides a rough estimate of our location," he said. *Assuming the signal made it beyond the mountains,* he thought, but there was no point in saying it.

"A rough estimate is better than nothing." Using a folded piece of cloth for a pot holder, Addie lifted the pan from the fire and filled the tin mugs with water.

Cole watched her, his stomach churning with anger and frustration. Anger at the situation and frustration at his own inability to do anything to change it. His head ached and his shoulder throbbed in vicious counterpoint. He wanted—needed—to do something to improve their situation, to bring them a step closer to rescue. And there wasn't a damned thing he could do.

How the hell could she sit there, making coffee as calmly as if she were in her kitchen? Must be that stiff-upper-lip thing the British were supposed to be so good at. Maybe it applied just as well to members of the upper class on this side of the pond, some side effect of having lots of money. He, on the other hand, came from a unashamedly middle-class background and he was in no mood to pretend that they were getting ready to take tea in the parlor.

Addie concentrated on keeping her hand steady as she added coffee to the hot water. She should have put the coffee into the cups first, she thought, watching the dark crystals float on top of the water before dispersing with sullen slowness. A sharp, earthy scent floated on the crisp mountain air. It had always seemed to her one of life's injustices that coffee smelled so much better than it tasted. The scent seemed to promise rich delight but the taste never delivered on that promise. It wasn't likely that this would prove the exception to the rule.

Not that it mattered, of course, but it was so much easier to think about the coffee than it was to think about what Cole had said. She picked up his cup and handed it to him.

"It isn't like they won't still be looking for us," she said, forcing a quick, meaningless little smile.

"They'll look," he agreed tiredly.

"Then we have to believe they'll find us."

Cole sipped his coffee and said nothing. There didn't seem to be anything to say in the face of her determined optimism. He should have been relieved that she'd taken the news so well. Instead he felt an irritation that was as unfair as it was irrational. What the hell did it take to get a reaction out of her?

The morning passed slowly. Addie pretended to read a novel she'd pulled from the ever fertile depths of her purse. Over the top of the book, she watched Cole. He was as restless as a cat, unable to settle in one place for more than a moment at a time.

He'd started out by circling the plane a couple of times, pausing to nudge something with his foot here, test something else with his hands there. He'd ducked inside and she'd seen him sitting in the cockpit a moment later, a stray sunbeam finding its way through the shattered windshield to pick out the gold in his hair. Now he was poking around in the Beech Craft's engine.

Addie chewed on her lower lip as she watched him. From the way he was favoring his shoulder, it was obvious that he was in more than a little pain and she was willing to bet that he was running a fever. His face was flushed, his eyes a little too bright. He should be resting, not working on a plane that even she could see was never going to fly again.

Not that he was likely to appreciate having that pointed out to him. In her admittedly limited experience, men rarely appreciated being offered any kind of advice. Her father certainly never expressed much interest in anyone else's opinion.

She tried to focus her attention on her book again, but after reading the same page three times without having the slightest idea of what she'd read, she gave up. Setting the book aside, she got up and limped over to the plane. Her ankle was still tender but it was improving. Cole glanced up as she approached. His expression was not particularly encouraging but the hectic flush in his cheeks stiffened Addie's determination to try to get him to sit down.

"I wondered if you'd like some more coffee," she said.

"No, thank you." Cole returned his attention to the engine.

Addie swallowed and decided she was going to have to try a more direct approach. "Your shoulder is bothering you, isn't it?"

"There's a hole in it," he said shortly. "It would be pretty strange if it didn't bother me."

"I think you're running a bit of a fever," she continued, ignoring his less than encouraging tone. When he didn't answer, she took a deep breath and stepped closer. "Cole, there's nothing you can do about the plane. Why don't you come and sit down. Let me take a look at your shoulder."

Cole was all but drowning in feelings of guilt and responsibility and her soft concern burned like acid against his skin. If she'd shouted at him, blamed him for their situation, he would have accepted that as no more than he deserved, but to have her worried about him was more than he could take. He spoke without looking at her, his voice low and hard.

"I know I'm running a fever and I know I can't fix the freaking plane and I also know we're stuck here and that there isn't a bloody thing I can do about it! But just in case I *hadn't* figured any of those things out, I really appreciate you pointing them out to me. Now, would you mind leaving me the bloody hell alone!"

The silence that followed could have been cut with a knife. It seemed as if even the birds caught their breath in shock. Cole closed his eyes and leaned his forehead against his arm, which was braced against the fuselage. The leather of his jacket felt cool against his hot skin. He heard the echo of his own harsh words and would have given almost anything to catch them back. *God, when had he become such a total jerk?*

"I'm sorry," she said, her voice thin and strained.

"Addie—" Cole lifted his head and stared at the chipped paint on the side of the plane. He didn't want to face her, didn't want to see the hurt he could so plainly hear.

"I shouldn't have . . . I didn't mean to . . . to bother you. I'm sorry."

"I'm the one who should apologize to you." He forced himself to turn and face her. She was pale and her eyes held a stricken expression that made Cole feel as if he'd just slapped her, which, in a way, was exactly what he'd done. He hadn't struck her physically but he'd lashed out at her verbally with every intention of hurting her.

"I—I didn't mean to bother you," she said again, her teeth worrying her lower lip. She eased back a step.

"You weren't bothering me. I had no business snarling at you like that." His conscience pinching viciously, he reached out and caught her wrist in his hand. "I acted like a jerk and I'm sorry."

"You were thinking and—"

"I was sulking," he corrected her.

"You've got a lot on your mind," she began, ready to excuse his behavior.

"Would you stop making excuses for me?" He shook her arm lightly, torn between exasperation and frustration. "I behaved like a prize bastard. There was absolutely no excuse and I'm sorry."

Addie stared at him, her blue eyes bewildered. "You didn't mean to upset—"

"Yes, I did." Cole released his hold on her wrist and stepped closer, bringing his hand up to cup his palm around the back of her neck. "I was totally in the wrong and I'm sorry."

"But—"

"No buts. Tell me you accept my apology or tell me to go to hell, but don't make excuses for me."

She stared up at him. Her teeth tugged at her lower lip and Cole had the whimsical thought that she was actually biting back another excuse for his behavior.

"I accept," she said finally, the words almost dragged from her.

"Thank you." Cole's smile was rueful. "I don't think I've ever had to work so hard to apologize. Hasn't anyone ever told you they were sorry before?"

"No," she said simply.

And that probably said a great deal about her past relationships, Cole thought. If she'd even *had* any past relationships. There was something...untouched about her. A sweetness and innocence that was rare in the world today. It was probably politically incorrect of him to find that innocence attractive.

The baby-fine curls on the nape of her neck tickled his hand. Cole's fingers shifted against her skin. He was suddenly sharply aware of her essential femininity. He couldn't help but remember the way she felt sleeping next to him, as trusting as a child. But there was nothing childish about the soft curves of her body. She might be small but she was all woman.

He stared down at her a moment longer. She had a very kissable mouth, he realized, and it was so close. He had only to lower his head for his mouth to touch hers; had only to move forward half a step to take her into his arms. Would she melt against him, as warm and soft as—

God, he had *lost his mind.* Shocked by the direction his thoughts had taken, Cole straightened abruptly, dropping his hand away from her neck and taking a half step back. He'd already decided that this was *not* going to happen.

Addie stared up at him, aware that her pulse was beating much too fast. There had been a moment there when she'd thought he was about to kiss her. She looked away, aware that her cheeks were flushed and hoping he wouldn't guess at the cause. It must have been her imagination. Not only did she find it difficult to imagine a man like Cole Walker *wanting* to kiss her, but if he *had* wanted to kiss her, he would have done so. *She* certainly wasn't going to offer any objections. How humiliating to think he might have realized that and still chose to step back!

"Well, if you know me very long, you'll probably hear quite a few apologies because I've got a miserable temper," Cole said, keeping his tone light with an effort.

"I don't believe that." Addie stepped back and Cole wondered if it was his imagination that she was flushed and looking a little self-conscious. As if she'd recognized his urge to kiss her. As if she might not have objected if he'd followed that urge?

Cole jerked his thoughts back into line. No matter how attractive he found her, he wasn't going to allow himself to forget that she was his responsibility.

The Family

Keefe had known Kel Bryan for ten years or more.
They'd met when both men were riding rodeo, chasing the promise of big gold buckles and fat purses on
the circuit. Kel had been born and raised on a ranch.
Keefe had grown up a stone's throw from Los Angeles, more familiar with the acrid bite of smog than
the crisp scent of sagebrush. But no one looking at
them would have been able to guess how different their
backgrounds were. Keefe Walker was every inch the
cowboy, from his boots to the battered Stetson hat he
wore.

They'd become friends on the circuit, competing
against one another in the ring, raising hell together
outside it. Celebrating wins and commiserating over
losses in honky-tonks and bars, drinking too much
and getting into more than a few brawls.

Kel left the circuit first, going home to Wyoming when his father died and left him with the responsibility of the Lazy B, making him the fourth generation of his family to tend the land. Keefe married, broke his leg, his wrist and his collarbone—twice—got a divorce, and looked to be well on his way to getting himself killed when he drew to an inside straight during a poker game in Missoula and found himself the owner of a broken-down ranch in California, providentially named The Flying Ace.

The two friends had stayed in touch in the desultory way of men more comfortable with action than words. There were no long, chatty phone calls and neither of them was inclined to write letters, but they touched base now and then, getting together whenever either one of them happened to be in the other's neighborhood—neighborhood being loosely defined to mean within a couple hundred miles. It was enough.

When Cole's plane went down in the mountains not too far from Kel's ranch, Keefe didn't hesitate to call him. He never doubted what Kel's response would be—any help he could give was Keefe's for the asking. When Keefe arrived at the Lazy B the second day after the plane's disappearance, Kel came out of the ranch house to meet him.

"You look like hell," he said by way of greeting.

"Wish I could say the same," Keefe said, grinning tiredly.

"Yeah, but I'm just getting better looking every year," Kel said with a grin.

"Must be quite a burden for your wife," Keefe commented.

"Megan bears up pretty well under the strain. Come on in and I'll introduce you."

Though Kel and Megan had been married for a couple of years, it was the first time Keefe had had a chance to meet her. His first impression was that she looked much too fragile to be a ranch wife. With her flaxen hair and delicate beauty, she looked like she'd be more at home being pampered in a beauty salon than living on a ranch miles from the nearest town. But her handshake was firm and there was strength in the thrust of her jaw and the steadiness of her gaze.

"I'm glad to finally get a chance to meet you," she said as they shook hands. Her smile was warm. "I'm sorry the circumstances aren't better."

"So am I."

"Are you the man who broke Daddy's nose?" The question came from belt buckle level.

"Michael! What a question!" Megan's scolding tone was spoiled by the hint of laughter. "Where are your manners?"

"Are you?" Michael asked, undeterred.

Keefe smiled down at his small questioner. Kel's son was the spitting image of his father, his green eyes meeting Keefe's straight-on. "Did your daddy tell you that I broke his nose?"

"Yep."

"Did he tell you how it happened?" Keefe asked, throwing his friend a wicked smile.

Kel made an unintelligible sound of protest. "Shouldn't you be helping Gracie fix lunch?"

"Gracie says I'm a nuisance in the kitchen," Michael announced with considerable pride. Then he promptly turned his attention back to his father's friend. "How come you broke Daddy's nose?"

Keefe shot another glance in Kel's direction, enjoying his friend's obvious discomfort. But when he answered Michael's question, he offered only the blandest of explanations. "It was an accident. Your dad tripped over...something and I was trying to break his fall. His nose got in the way of my fist."

"Oh." Michael small face was puckered in a disappointed frown. Clearly, he'd been hoping for something more exciting than this plebeian explanation.

"Why don't you go wash up before lunch?" Megan told her son. "Mr. Walker will be eating with us," she added when the boy hesitated. Satisfied that the interesting new stranger wasn't going to disappear, Michael dashed off, his small boots clattering on the hardwood floors. Megan looked at Kel, raising one slim brow in question. "Your nose got in the way of his fist?"

"It's a long story," Kel said, looking uneasy.

"Give me the abridged version."

Kel shot Keefe a harassed look but rescue came from another direction. A thin but demanding wail floated down the stairs. "Hannah's awake," Kel said, his voice holding unconcealed gratitude for the interruption provided by his six-month-old daughter.

"I'll get her." Megan started toward the stairs but paused to fix her husband with a mock stern look. "I still want to hear this story."

Kel watched her until she was out of sight and then turned a disgruntled look in Keefe's direction. "My nose got in the way of your fist? Couldn't you come up with something better than that?"

"Well, I guess I could have told him that you were drunker than a waltzing pissant and putting the moves on the prettiest waitress in Tulsa and that if I hadn't punched you, her boyfriend would have torn your head off and handed it to you on a platter," Keefe drawled.

"I could have handled him," Kel protested automatically.

"Not even if you were sober." Keefe shook his head. "If you'd managed to pull your eyes away from his girlfriend's cleavage, you'd might have noticed that he had hands like hams."

"So you say." They'd had this same discussion on more than one occasion, starting the morning Kel woke with a hangover and a broken nose. A knock on the front door interrupted the discussion.

"That will be Lije," Kel said as he went to answer it. "He's the pilot I told you about."

At the reminder of why he was here, the smile left Keefe's eyes, his expression turning grim as he moved forward to meet Lije Blackhawk, one of Kel's cowboys who also happened to be a helicopter pilot. Kel had arranged to borrow a helicopter from a neighboring ranch and Lije had agreed to run a search pattern over the area where Cole had last made radio contact.

As the three men bent over a map laid out on the desk in Kel's office, Keefe renewed the promise he'd made to himself and to his family: he was going to find his brother. No matter what it took, he wasn't going home without Cole. He just hoped to God that he'd find him alive.

Chapter 5

Four days. Cole scratched four stripes in the dirt with a stick and stared at them unseeingly. It had been four days since he'd been forced to set the plane down. Four days without any sign of a search plane. The only evidence they'd had that they weren't the only people left on the planet was the occasional jet trail that arrowed across the pale winter sky.

He narrowed his eyes as he stared down the slope of the mountain. It would have been helpful to have some idea of where they were, maybe a rough estimate of how far it was to the nearest outpost of civilization. If they could walk out... He shook his head. Addie's ankle was much better but she wasn't up to doing any serious hiking, especially not wearing a pair of loafers. And honesty compelled him to admit that he wasn't exactly up to par yet, either. The fever had disappeared last night but his shoulder still hurt like hell if he moved incautiously.

It would be a few days before they could even think about trying to walk out and even then... He just didn't know. Leaving the plane would be risky. Not only because of the shelter it provided if the weather turned ugly, though that could be significant. But his main concern was that the plane was visible from the air. The crisp blue and white of the fuselage stood out against the duns and greens of the mountainside and their best hope of being found lay in staying with the plane. If there was any hope of being found at all.

"You look like you're contemplating the fate of nations," Addie said as she walked toward him.

"Not nations. Unless we want to declare ourselves independent and establish a new capitol."

He accepted the cup she handed him. Since they were trying to stretch their supplies as much as possible, the coffee was little more than tinted water but it was hot, which was enough to make it, not only acceptable, but downright welcome. Though the sky remained clear, the temperature had dropped and not even the clear sunlight could disguise the chill in the air.

"Think we're going to have snow?" he asked, tilting his head toward the clouds that were gathering along the tops of the mountains.

Addie followed his gaze and a faint, worried frown creased her forehead. "It kind of looks that way, doesn't it?"

"We should be okay inside the plane," he said. "Unless it's a major blizzard."

Addie shrugged one shoulder. "Even if it is, there's nothing we can do to stop it."

"Are you always so philosophical or is it just major disaster that brings out this tendency?" he asked conversationally.

Addie shrugged again, a fleeting smile curving her mouth. "I just don't see much sense in getting upset about things I can't change."

"Logical," Cole agreed, nodding. "Guaranteed to annoy those of us with weaker reasoning, but it's undeniably logical."

Addie laughed and shook her head. "I don't think there's anything weak about your reasoning."

She moved back up the slope to where the fire burned. Cole watched her go and thought, not for the first time, that he was lucky to have been marooned with her. The past few days hadn't been a walk in the park but they could have been hell on earth if he'd been stuck with almost anyone else. Of course, the situation was not without its disadvantages, Cole admitted as Addie leaned over to add a stick to the fire. The movement pulled the khaki cotton of her slacks taut across her rounded bottom and made him think any number of things he had no business thinking.

With an effort, he dragged his gaze away from her. When they got back to civilization, he could feel free to pursue this unexpected attraction, he promised himself. *If* they got back to civilization, he added, casting an uneasy glance at the clouds piling up along the tops of the mountains.

* * *

Cole started awake, his pulse thrumming. The first thing he was aware of was that he was cold. He was sitting on the ground, his back propped against a rock. When he'd dozed off, the sun had been shining and the fire had been casting out a pleasant warmth. He hadn't been what he'd call warm, but he'd been comfortable. Now the sun was gone, the fire had died down until it was nothing more than a sullenly smoldering pile of ash and coals, and he was chilled all the way to his bones.

He sat up, groaning as his back announced its displeasure in his choice of beds. Considering the way he'd been slumped against the rock, it was a wonder his back wasn't broken. Come to think of it, maybe it *was* broken, he thought as he stood and straightened his spine cautiously. A glance at his watch told him that he'd been asleep for a couple of hours. No wonder he was so stiff.

He felt like Dorothy Gale, only instead of waking in the colorful land of Oz, he'd awakened in the black-and-white world of Kansas. Maybe not Kansas, he conceded, glancing at the mountains that loomed above him, but the black-and-white part of it certainly fit. While he slept, the clouds had crept across the sky, stretching from peak to peak in a thick canopy. His watch said that an hour or more remained until sunset but the light held the still, gray quality of dusk, bleaching the color from everything it touched. There was a dry, almost sharp taste to the air that spoke of snow, even to his Southern California-bred senses.

His frown deepened as he looked around the make-shift campsite. Where was Addie? She'd been sitting on the other side of the fire reading when he fell asleep. Her book was lying facedown on the ground but she was gone. His first thought was that she'd just gone to answer a call of nature, but the fire obviously hadn't been fed in quite a while. Maybe she was in the plane?

But she wasn't in the plane. Nor did she answer when he called her name.

That didn't mean that something had happened to her, Cole told himself. He stood next to the dying fire, his feet braced apart, hand on his hip, his dark eyes scanning the surrounding area for some clue to Addie's whereabouts. Maybe she'd just gone for a walk and lost track of time.

Yeah, right. She went tramping off into the wilderness with a bum ankle and a storm coming on.

It took him thirty minutes to find her. With every minute that passed, his imagination presented him with increasingly gruesome explanations for her disappearance, everything from falling down a mine shaft to drowning in the little stream that had been providing them with water.

The light, which hadn't been particularly good to start with, continued to fade and Cole cursed the fact that he hadn't thought to bring the flashlight from the plane.

"Addie?" He'd been calling her name at regular intervals and had nearly given up hope of getting a response.

"Here."

For a moment Cole thought he'd imagined it, that his need for a response had conjured up the faint sound of her voice.

"Addie?"

"I'm here." Her voice was louder this time, strained with the effort of projecting it. "Don't go away. I'm here."

Cole followed the sound of her voice and found himself slipping and sliding down a steep slope. He dug the heels of his boots into the layer of pine needles and fallen twigs to control his descent. The slope ended in a sharp drop-off, and he guessed that, in better light, there would probably be a spectacular view from where he stood. But he wasn't interested in the view at the moment.

"Where the hell are you?" he demanded, scowling into the gloom.

"Down here." Her voice seemed to come from under his feet.

"Holy—" Cole bit off a curse as he realized where she must be.

A heartbeat later he leaned over the edge of the cliff and stared down into Addie's frightened eyes. She was standing on a narrow ledge that jutted out about eight feet down from the lip of the drop-off.

"I fell," she said, as if feeling an explanation was necessary.

"No kidding. And here I was thinking you'd gotten the urge for a little rock climbing. Are you hurt?"

"N-no. I don't think so. My ankle hurts and I lost one of my...shoes." Her voice hitched on the last word, giving him a pretty good idea of just how scared she was. But she sucked in a sharp breath and almost visibly grabbed hold of her self-control. "I'm okay," she said firmly.

"You'll be better when we get you off that ledge." Cole started to pull back from the edge.

"Don't leave me!" Addie cried, her voice thin with panic.

Cole stopped immediately. "It's okay," he said soothingly. "I'm not going anywhere. I just need to figure out how to haul you up. I'm not going to leave you."

"I know. I'm sorry. I know you're not going to leave me." Addie leaned her forehead against the cold rock face of the mountain and closed her eyes for a moment. She fought down the panic that had ripped through her when he'd moved out of sight. Of course he wasn't going to leave her. She tilted her head back and looked up at him. "I'm okay. It's just that I've been down here a long time and I... But I'm okay now."

"I'll be right back," Cole said, looking less than reassured.

"I'm okay," she insisted, forcing a smile and then having to catch back a cry of terror when he pulled back. But he wasn't gone long.

"Here." Cole's face appeared above her again. "Slip this over your wrist."

It wasn't until she'd grabbed hold of it that Addie realized she held one end of his belt. He'd threaded the end through the buckle, pulling it down until it formed a small loop. With fingers made clumsy by the cold, she managed to slide the stiff leather over her hand, feeling the loop settle around her narrow wrist.

"Grab hold of it with your other hand and don't let go. I'll pull you up."

"What about your shoulder?"

Cole's response was short and pungent. His face vanished without waiting for a response and a moment later Addie saw the thin strip of his belt grow taut across the rock face and then felt the loop bite into her wrist as he began to pull her up. Though it couldn't have taken more than a couple of minutes, Addie felt as if she spent a lifetime dangling against the cliff face with nothing but Cole's strength between her and eternity.

It occurred to her afterward that she hadn't been nearly as frightened as she should have been. It might have been because she was simply too numb to feel any more fear, but when she thought about it later she realized that she'd simply never doubted that Cole would bring her safely out of danger.

Cole didn't share her confidence in his ability. Flat on his belly on the winter-cold ground, he pulled Addie up the cliff face. Half-forgotten prayers skittered through his mind, mixed with a few more profane thoughts and a stubborn determination to win the battle. Every muscle in his body strained with the effort of supporting her dead weight. Pain stabbed through his injured shoulder and he knew that the wound had torn open, but it was a distant, unimportant thing. All that mattered was seeing her safe.

Another few inches, a foot, two feet. And then he could see her hand, her fingers digging into the ground, scrabbling for purchase. Gritting his teeth, Cole pulled her up a few more inches.

Almost. Almost. There.

His hand closed around her wrist and she was dragged the rest of the way up in a quick rush that startled a cry from her.

Addie had never realized how wonderful the cold, hard ground could feel. There were pine needles digging into her cheek, she'd lost one shoe, her stocking-clad foot was frozen and her left arm felt as if it had been pulled half out its socket. But those were minor complaints compared to the sheer delight of being on solid ground. If it hadn't been for Cole...

She started to lift her head to look at him, knowing that there was nothing she could say to express her gratitude. But before she could find the words to try to express her thanks, hard fingers closed over her shoulders and she found herself dragged upward until she was on her knees, facing her rescuer. But he looked more in the mood for murder than gratitude.

"What the hell were you doing?" he demanded in a tone that managed to combine both a growl and a shout.

"D-doing?"

"Were you trying to kill yourself?" His fingers tightened on her shoulders and she had the distinct impression that he was barely restraining the urge to shake her until her teeth rattled.

"I—I was taking a w-walk," she stammered, bewildered by his reaction.

"Off a fifty-foot cliff?" he demanded.

"No. It was...I slipped and—"

But she didn't get a chance to finish her explanation. Her breasts collided with the hard muscles of Cole's chest and her breath was stolen by the hot pressure of his mouth on hers.

Cole's kiss was sharp with temper and sweetened by hunger and relief. If she'd had more experience with men, Addie might have recognized his reaction for what it was—a classic male response to having been frightened. But the only man she knew well was her father and he was not a man of strong emotional reactions. Even his anger was cold and controlled—more ice than fire.

There was certainly nothing cold about Cole. He was all heat and passion and Addie felt the impact of his kiss all the way down to her toes. None of her fantasies had prepared her for this. She'd imagined him kissing her tenderly, wooing her gently. Instead his mouth devoured hers. He wasn't asking for her response but demanding her total surrender. And she was willing to give him exactly what he wanted, she realized dazedly. She dissolved into the embrace, her mouth opening to his, her fingers digging into the solid muscles of his shoulders as she let herself be swept up into the whirlwind.

Ironically, the feel of her body curving to his, the soft hunger of her response served to snap Cole back to an awareness of time and place. He dragged his mouth from hers and stared down at her, his dark eyes holding an expression not much different than the shock in Addie's. His breathing was ragged, his heart thudding against his breastbone. He wanted to believe it was a residual effect of the physical effort he'd put in to pulling her to safety. That's what he *wanted* to believe, but he knew it was something more elemental than that.

They stared at each other for the space of several heartbeats. Between them was the subconscious awareness that they stood on the brink of a precipice every bit as dangerous as the one beside them. Tension hummed between them like a tautly drawn rope.

It was Cole who shattered the moment, releasing her and standing abruptly. "It's getting dark," he said. His tone was flat and calm, as if the last few minutes hadn't happened. "We should get back to the plane."

"Yes." Addie started to stand, trying to look as if his kiss hadn't shaken her to the core, as if her knees weren't weak from its effects. She'd barely gained her feet when Cole bent and, without a word, swept her up into his arms, startling a shocked gasp from her.

"I can walk," she said hastily.

"Not without a shoe." Cole moved up the slope with a surefootedness that belied the burden he carried.

"Your shoulder—" she began.

"Shut. Up." He didn't raise his voice but there was something in the way he made each word separate and distinct from the other that made Addie decide that this wasn't the time to assert her independence.

Lying silent in his arms, she could feel the steady thud of his heart beneath her cheek. It was a reassuring sound. She didn't understand why Cole had kissed her the way he had. She didn't know why he seemed angry with her yet was carrying her with such gentle concern. But, for the moment, she didn't care about anything except that she was safe and he was holding her.

It began to snow as they reached the top of the slope. It started slowly. Not a howling blizzard but a deceptively gentle fall, crystalline flakes drifting downward to paint every surface with lacy patterns of ethereal beauty. Cole bit back a curse and increased his pace as much as he could, considering there was barely enough light left to see to put one foot in front of the other. By the time they reached the plane, the ground was covered by a thin white blanket.

He set Addie down inside the plane and then went back out to gather up the things that had been left outside. He brought everything inside, cast one last, unappreciative look at the softly pretty snowfall and pulled the Beech Craft's door closed, shutting the storm out. And them in.

With the door closed, the darkness inside the plane was almost complete. Cole made his way to where they'd stacked their supplies and found the candles that had been a part of his camping gear. They hadn't used them before this, choosing to let the sun set the pattern of their days. But he was in no mood to sit in the dark tonight.

He could feel Addie watching him as he lit the candles and set them in the center of an aluminum plate. He didn't look at her. He knew he should say something—offer an apology, an explanation. But an apology seemed almost insultingly inadequate and what could he offer by way of explanation? There *was* no explanation. He stared at the flickering candle flames and tried to figure out how he'd managed to lose control of himself the way he had.

"Did you hurt your shoulder?" Addie's calm question broke the taut silence that had prevailed for the past twenty minutes.

Calling himself a coward, Cole seized on the opportunity to postpone explanations for which he could find no words.

"I think I tore it open," he admitted. Since he could feel the blood sticking his shirt to his back, "think" wasn't entirely accurate.

"Let me look at it."

Cole hesitated. The last thing he wanted was to have her looking at his injury, taking care of him, acting as if he hadn't behaved like a bastard when he'd kissed her. On the other hand, it didn't make much sense to keep his pride intact while he bled to death. Cursing his injured shoulder, his temper, the weather and the fact that they were here in the first place, he began unbuttoning his coat.

"It doesn't look too bad," Addie announced a few minutes later.

"Good." Cole stared at the curving wall opposite him and wrestled with his feelings. It was nearly as cold inside the plane as it was outside and goose bumps rose across his bare torso. His shoulder hurt almost as much as it had when he'd first injured it but he wasn't concerned with his physical discomforts. Far more painful was the vicious pinch of his conscience. The more he thought about the way he'd treated Addie, the worse he felt. He'd never manhandled a woman in his life. And to do that to Addie of all people...

"That should do," she said, breaking into his guilty contemplation.

"Thanks." He rose and went to get a clean shirt. Since they'd intended to spend the night in South Dakota, they each had a change of clothes with them. The shirt Cole picked up now was the one he'd been wearing the day of the crash. Ice-cold water from the stream had served to take the worst of the bloodstains out but the blue chambray was stiff, torn in several places and hopelessly wrinkled. He contemplated it without enthusiasm for a moment before sliding his arms into the sleeves.

"This trip has been rough on my wardrobe," he muttered, speaking half to himself.

"I lost my shoe." Addie's tone was so mournful that Cole turned to look at her.

She was sitting on the air mattress, one foot tucked under the opposite leg, the other foot stuck out in front of her. She stared at her stocking-clad foot as sadly as if she were contemplating a deceased friend.

"You'll be able to get a new pair," Cole said, surprised that the loss of a shoe seemed to bother her so much. She hadn't looked this upset when he told her the EMT wasn't working. He finished pulling his shirt on, favoring his injured shoulder.

"I—I liked this pair." Her voice caught on a half sob.

"It could have been worse," he offered, at a loss to understand her distress.

She was silent a moment and he thought she'd regained her usual calm. But the eyes she lifted to his face were bleak and wet with tears. "We're going to die here, aren't we?"

"No!" One long stride brought him to her. He dropped to his knees next to her. "We are not going to die here."

"You can't know that." A single tear slid down her cheek but her eyes held a quiet acceptance that cut him to the quick.

"I do know it," he lied. His voice was sharp but his hands were gentle on her upper arms.

"No, you don't," she said sadly. "We don't even know if anyone is looking for us."

"My family will be looking," Cole said instantly.

"You can't know that."

"Stop telling me what I can't know," he told her. "You don't know my family, but I do, and I know they'll be looking for us and they won't stop until they find us." He tightened his grip on her arms and shook her gently. "Hey, what happened to the woman who's been treating a plane crash like it's a walk in the park? Where's that philosophical attitude that drives me nuts?"

Addie stared at him, her lip quivering in a way that made Cole's heart nearly crack. "I think I lost it when I lost my shoe," she said as mournful as a child.

A second tear joined the first and then he had her in his arms, her cheek pressed to his bare chest.

The last person who'd held Addie while she cried was her mother. Since her death when Addie was fourteen, any tears had been shed alone. Her father had no patience with tears, considering them a waste of time. If Cole had reacted with the same irritation, Addie might have been able to force back her tears. But the wordless comfort of his hold shattered the brittle shell of control that she'd so carefully built around herself since the crash. Her breath caught on a gulping sob and her body went slack in his arms.

"I'm sorry," she got out between sobs.

"Hush." Cole shifted their positions, lifting her with easy strength and settling her across his thighs so that she lay cradled against his body. "It's all right," he murmured. He rubbed his hand over her trembling back, his voice a soothing rumble in her ear.

The cliché was that a woman's tears turned even the strongest man into a gibbering idiot, but Cole hadn't spent nearly seven years as a single father for nothing. Gut instinct told him that Addie's tears were caused by too much worry, too little sleep and more than a little stress. She wasn't crying over the loss of her shoe, nor even because she believed they were going to die. Her tears were the result of tension. He treated her the same way he would have treated Mary—he let her cry it out.

Addie cried until she had no tears left. She was aware of Cole holding her, of the soft murmur of his voice, the gentle stroke of his hand, the solid warmth of his body against hers. By the time her tears slowed to an occasional hiccuping sob, she felt completely drained.

"Feel better?" Cole asked.

"Yes." She was surprised to realize it was the truth. Her nose was stuffed up, her throat was clogged, her breath hitched in the middle and her body ached as if she'd just run a marathon, but despite all that, she felt better.

"Good." He tilted her face up and dried her cheeks with the tail of the shirt he'd taken off earlier. "Blow."

"That's your shirt," she protested.

"It washes. Blow." It was probably the same tone he would have used with his daughter, Addie thought. Even at twenty-seven, she recognized that there was no arguing with it. She blew.

Tossing the shirt away, Cole cupped her chin in his hand, tilting her face up to his. "We are not going to die."

"Okay," she agreed. She was too tired to argue. Besides, with Cole holding her like this, death seemed a distant concept.

"They're looking for us right now. Even if search and rescue gives up, my brothers won't."

"You sound awfully sure of that."

"We're family," he said simply, as if that explained everything.

Perhaps it did, if you were one of the Walkers. Addie tried—and failed—to imagine her father trekking into the mountains in search of her. Ronald Smith might endure, without hesitation, any amount of discomfort and inconvenience during the course of an archaeological dig but it would never occur to him to get involved in any rescue operations.

It's always best to allow the experts to do their jobs and trust that they do them well. Remember that it's a waste of time to second-guess a man in his own field, Adelaide.

No, whatever Cole's family might do, her father wouldn't be involved.

Cole's thumb brushed across her damp cheek and it occurred to Addie that she probably looked like hell. She was not one of those lucky women who could cry without her eyes getting puffy and her skin flushing as if she had a fatal fever. Not even candlelight could completely conceal the ravages of her tears. But if Cole found anything objectionable about the way she looked, it didn't show.

"I'm sorry about the way I acted before," he said quietly. "I behaved like a jackass. I shouldn't have kissed you like that."

Sorry for kissing her or only for the way he'd kissed her? Addie wondered. Her eyes searched his, but with the candles behind him, his face was all shadows and angles, his expression unreadable.

"Do you think I could try it again?" Cole answered the question she hadn't had the courage to ask. His voice was low and husky, as soft as a caress, and Addie felt a shiver slide down her spine.

"Behave like a jackass?" she asked, only half-aware of her own words.

Cole's teeth flashed in a quick grin. "I thought I'd skip that and go straight to the kissing part. If you don't mind?"

Addie groped frantically for the appropriate response but her mind remained resolutely empty. *Say something, nitwit!* He was asking if he could kiss her and all she could do was stare up at him like a dead carp in a fish market. But perhaps he read the answer in her eyes because his head bent to hers.

His mouth touched hers in a kiss as soft as the first one had been hard. He made no demands this time but instead coaxed a response from her, his mouth teasing hers into opening to him. He deepened the kiss gradually, his tongue stroking her lower lip before delving inside to taste the sweet honey of her mouth.

Addie surrendered completely, her hands came up, her fingers gripping little handfuls of his open shirt, clinging to it as the world slowly dipped and swayed around her. It wasn't the first time she'd been kissed but it was the first time she'd felt as if her bones were in danger of dissolving.

Cole tightened his arms around her, ignoring the warning twinge from his shoulder. He'd known this was how she'd feel, how she'd taste. She felt so right in his arms, as if he'd held her like this before, kissed her like this before. As if what was happening was inevitable, destined by fate.

The thought shook him. Simple desire was one thing. There was no mystery about stark male hunger. But there was something deeper here. He had the sense of standing on the edge of a cliff, the view below obscured by mist. A misstep now could lead to something he'd regret—something they might both regret.

It took a concentrated effort to loosen his arms around Addie and, even then, her soft sigh of protest was almost his undoing. Her lashes, still damp with tears, lifted slowly and she stared up at him with dazed blue eyes. Cole felt his body tighten at the desire she so openly revealed. It didn't seem to occur to her to hide what she was feeling. There was no subterfuge, no coy pretending. He'd never realized how erotic honesty could be.

"This isn't the time or the place," he said slowly, his voice full of regret. "We're both worn-out and half-frozen. You're exhausted and I'm not exactly up to par."

As he spoke, he was gently prying her fingers away from his open shirtfront and easing her off his lap and back down onto the air mattress. "Things may look different in the morning," he said, just before leaning over to blow out the candles.

Addie lay in the darkness, listening to the soft rustling sounds as he took off his boots. A moment later he was lying next to her, pulling her back against him in the sleeping position they'd adopted over the past few nights. She let her body curl into his.

He was right—she was cold and the day's events had left her exhausted to the bone. But as for things looking different in the morning, she couldn't imagine a time when she wouldn't want him to hold her and kiss her.

Though she wouldn't have believed it possible, Addie slept deeply and dreamlessly. Her mind might have been inclined to ponder everything that had happened, but her body was simply too exhausted to care. She fell asleep almost immediately, Cole's arm draped over her, pulling her back against the heat of his much larger body.

She was awakened with painful abruptness when Cole threw back the sleeping bag covering them and lunged from the bed. She heard him say something as he stepped over her.

"What?" By the time she sat up, he was at the plane's door and wrenching it open.

"Chopper." The single word drifted back to her and then he was outside.

Chopper? Her head spinning with the abrupt shift from sleeping to waking, Addie stared blankly after him for a moment. He'd gone out without his shoes. Why would he— A low thrumming sound penetrated her sleep-fogged brain. A helicopter. Oh, my God, it was a helicopter! Scrambling up, she ran for the door, ignoring the protests from her injured ankle. There was a helicopter!

Sunlight reflecting off snow nearly blinded her as she stepped out of the plane. The storm had moved on during the night, leaving a pristine blanket of white to cover every surface. The clouds had disappeared and the sun poured down out of a clear blue sky. Addie was oblivious to the crisp beauty of it. Putting a hand up to shield her eyes, she looked up, seeking the source of that wonderful, magical sound.

"Help me clear the plane," Cole said sharply.

She turned and saw that he was sweeping the snow from the plane, using a broken pine branch to extend his reach.

"The plane will be visible from the air," he said when she didn't immediately respond to his demand.

Realizing what he meant, Addie looked around for a branch with which to help him. The bright colors of the plane would stand out against the snow. It was the work of a few moments to clear the light dusting of snow from the wrecked aircraft. When it was done, there was nothing to do but wait. And listen. And pray.

She hadn't seen the helicopter yet but she could hear it. The low thrumming grew louder and then terrified her by receding.

"He's running a close search pattern," Cole muttered, speaking to himself as much as to Addie. "He doesn't know what he's looking for. The plane might have broken up on impact."

"What if he doesn't come this way?"

"He will."

Addie looked at him, wondering if he had some concrete knowledge that he could sound so sure.

Cole caught her look and smiled grimly. "He has to."

The sound grew louder and Addie reached out, her fingers biting into his arm as they waited, unmoving, hardly breathing. Sound echoed off the mountains, making it difficult to pinpoint the source. There was a heart-stopping moment when the sound seemed to fade to nothing. He'd missed them, Addie thought, her throat nearly closing with despair. He'd gone the other way and missed them.

And then the chopper was there, swinging around the shoulder of the mountain and swooping down on them. The sound of the rotors was earsplittingly loud. Addie thought she'd never heard anything so beautiful in her life.

Cole moved away from the plane and waved his arms over his head, but it was clear that the pilot had already seen them. Addie followed him, oblivious to the rocks that dug into her stockinged feet and the snow that chilled them. The chopper swooped lower, seeming almost to dip and nod in acknowledgment of them before moving up again.

"They found us," Cole said, shouting to be heard over the roar of the chopper's rotors. "They found us!"

Without waiting for her response, he caught her up in his arms, swinging her around in a gesture of pure exuberance. Laughing, Addie threw her arms around his neck, giddy with happiness. When Cole's mouth came down on hers, it seemed the most natural thing in the world. Suspended in his arms, she returned the kiss, sharing his joy, celebrating life.

When he lifted his mouth from hers, he looked down at her for a long moment, his eyes searching even as he smiled. "This is getting to be a habit. I'm going to have to watch that."

Then the chopper swooped lower and he set her down before Addie could find the words to tell him that she'd rather he didn't watch it, that she'd like nothing better than for kissing her to become a habit of his.

The Family

Whoever had first said that waiting was hell had known what they were talking about, Keefe thought. He rubbed the curry brush over the back of a sleek little chestnut mare, his movements automatic. He'd flown to Wyoming because he didn't want to sit on his hands in Santa Barbara, waiting for word on his brother. But he hadn't been able to do much more than that here.

For the last two days Lije Blackhawk had taken the helicopter into the mountains to the east. Keefe's first thought had been that he should go up with him but the less weight the chopper carried, the farther Lije could go before he had to refuel. So Keefe stayed on the Lazy B and waited. The official searches had yielded nothing so far and neither had Lije. Though he was reluctant to admit it, Keefe knew that with every day that passed, the odds of finding Cole safe and sound crept a little bit lower.

"Waiting is sheer hell, isn't it?"

"Worse than a root canal," Keefe agreed, turning as Kel's wife approached. Her pale hair seemed to catch and hold the sunlight that spilled in through the open barn door.

"You're doing everything you can."

"Yeah, grooming horses is going to make a big difference in finding my brother," he said, one corner of his mouth turning down in a self-deprecating smile.

"Maybe not, but since there isn't anything else you can do, it's better than nothing." She came farther into the barn and Keefe realized that she was carrying the baby.

"Isn't it kind of cold for her?" he asked, setting down the curry brush and coming forward.

"You sound like Kel," Megan said. "If he had his way, she'd never be allowed out of the house in anything less than a Charlie Brown snowsuit."

"A Charlie Brown snowsuit?" Keefe questioned, moving close enough to peer down into the baby's face.

"You know, one of those snowsuits that has so many layers that the poor kid can't move without assistance. I can't convince Kel that she's not as breakable as she looks."

"Well, she isn't very big."

"Yeah, but she's tough, aren't you, sweetie?" The infant smiled up at her mother and waved her little arms in the air, babbling something that could have been agreement.

Kel didn't argue but he couldn't think of any word less applicable to Hannah Rose Bryan than "tough." He'd made her acquaintance the first night he was on the Lazy B. At six months, she ruled her world with a toothless smile and a truly awe-inspiring lung capacity. All silky red hair and eyes starting to turn as green as her father's, Keefe couldn't remember seeing a prettier baby.

"She's going to be a heartbreaker someday," he said now, grinning down at her. He brushed her cheek with the tip of his finger. "Look at that smile."

"She already is," Megan said ruefully, seeing the blatant infatuation on Keefe's face. "Would you like to hold her?"

Keefe showed none of the hesitation typical of a bachelor offered the chance to hold an infant. He lifted Hannah from her mother's arms, holding her with easy competence.

"How are you, huh?" Hannah stared up at him, her eyes wide and round as she considered him. Apparently deciding that he was worthy of being a member of her devoted court, she awarded him a smile. Keefe grinned down at her, his heart dropping neatly into her tiny hands.

"You seem to be pretty comfortable with infants," Megan commented.

"I have a niece. We all spoiled her rotten when she was a baby." Keefe's smile faded. "Cole's little girl." He handed Hannah back to her mother, the momentary lightness of spirit vanishing.

"There's something about a baby that makes all things seem possible," Megan said, cuddling her daughter. Her eyes were warm with compassion. "You have to believe Lije will find him."

"Yeah." Keefe only hoped he found Cole still alive.

As if on cue, the sound of a helicopter drifted into the barn. Keefe's eyes met Megan's, his gut clenching as tight as his fists.

"He's back early," Megan said, expressing the thought in both their minds.

Lije *was* early, Keefe thought as he brushed past her and went out the door. Barring a problem with the helicopter, there was only one thing that would bring him back to the Lazy B before he had to refuel. He'd found something.

By the time he'd circled the barn, Lije was setting the chopper down in the area that functioned as a landing pad. Keefe kept his mind a perfect blank as he watched the craft settle to the ground, all its airborne grace disappearing, making it appear heavy and ungainly. He was vaguely aware of Megan following him from the barn. Out of the corner of his eye, he could see Kel leaving the house where he'd spent the morning working on the books. Kel would have heard the sound of the chopper and known what it must mean.

Keefe moved forward, his long stride even, his expression as blank as his thoughts. He couldn't even assemble a coherent prayer. The chopper door opened and Lije dropped to the ground. But instead of ducking under the rotors and moving away from the aircraft, he turned back.

Keefe's heart stopped when Lije lifted his arms as if to help someone out of the chopper. He'd found them and at least one of them was alive. The first figure was much smaller than Cole—a woman. The passenger, Addie Smith. Keefe registered her presence only peripherally as Lije stepped back. And then a tall, familiar figure dropped to the ground and Keefe broke into a run.

Cole. Thank God. It was Cole and he was alive.

Chapter 6

"I don't think I'll ever be able to take hot showers for granted again," Addie said. She rubbed a thick blue towel over her still damp hair and gave her hostess a shy smile. "I really appreciate the way you've opened your home to us. You've been very kind."

"I'm not doing anything extraordinary," Megan said, brushing her thanks aside with a quick smile. "Anyone else would have done the same. Now, I've brought you some clothes. I think we're close enough to the same size that they should fit you. I wasn't sure what you'd like so I brought some things for you to choose from."

"I like anything I haven't been wearing for the past few days," Addie assured her.

"I can certainly understand that." Megan's smile was warm. "Kel's idea of camping involves hiking into

the mountains with nothing but a change of under-
wear and a hunting knife to fend off stray grizzlies.
But my idea of roughing it is staying in a motel where
the TV doesn't work. He dragged me along on a
camping trip once but my favorite part was getting
home and taking a nice hot shower."

Addie laughed. Though she'd met Megan Bryan
barely an hour ago, she felt as if she'd known her a lot
longer. From the moment she'd stepped out of the
helicopter, Megan had welcomed her as if she were an
old friend.

Things had moved so quickly over the past few
hours. From the moment she and Cole had awakened
to the rhythmic sound of the helicopter rotors, time
had seemed to speed up, sweeping her up in its current and tumbling her headlong. Leaving the crash site
had been so simple as to be almost anticlimactic. The
helicopter set down and the pilot got out. He'd intro-
duced himself as Lije Blackhawk, said he worked for
a friend of Cole's brother Keefe and that he was
damned glad to see both of them alive and well. Cole
had laughed and said he couldn't be half as glad to see
them as they were to see him. Then she and Cole had
gathered their few belongings together and the three
of them got in the shiny silver helicopter. When it took
off, they were officially rescued.

It had been a relatively short trip to Kel Bryan's
ranch, not nearly long enough for Addie to make the
mental adjustment from plane crash survivor to res-
cuee. When Lije set the chopper down and she saw
people approaching them, she'd felt a flutter of panic
at the thought of being back in civilization again. It

was promptly followed by a spurt of amusement as she considered the classic "wide open spaces" that surrounded the ranch. Calling this "civilization" required a considerable stretch of imagination. But knowing that didn't still her uneasiness. And then Megan had put her arm around her, her pretty gray eyes full of tears as she hugged her and welcomed her home and Addie had forgotten about her uneasiness.

Sometimes friendships took years to develop and sometimes they took only a moment.

"Did Cole get hold of his family?" Addie asked. She draped the towel over her shoulder and snugged the belt of her borrowed robe tighter around her waist.

"He just got off the phone with them," Megan said. "They were all at his brother's house so he was able to talk to them all."

"I'm glad. I know he was very worried about them, especially about his little girl."

"From what he said before he went to take a shower, I gather they're all just fine. Mary told him that she wasn't worried because her uncle Keefe had told her that he'd bring Cole back. Apparently, as far as she's concerned, that's all the reassurance anyone could want."

Addie smiled but she thought she knew how Mary felt. Cole had a way of making you believe what he said. She didn't know Keefe, but if he shared his younger brother's ability to inspire confidence, she wasn't surprised that Mary had believed him.

"I'm glad Cole was able to reach them," she said.

"So am I." Megan glanced at the clock on the dresser. "I'd better go help Gracie with supper. Lije is going to fly you to the airport in an hour and a half and I want to send you off with some food in your stomach.''

''I don't want to put you to any trouble,'' Addie began, but a comically loud grumble from her stomach interrupted her. She looked at Megan, her face flushed with embarrassment. Megan grinned, her eyes sparkling with humor.

''*You* may not want to put me to any trouble but I don't think your stomach feels half as noble.''

''Actually, my stomach feels like my throat's been cut,'' Addie admitted, her embarrassment vanishing beneath the warmth in Megan's smile.

''By the time you finish dressing and come downstairs, supper should be on the table,'' Megan promised her. With another quick smile, she left Addie alone.

Megan was as good as her word. Half an hour later, when Addie came downstairs, she was able to follow her nose to the dining room. The room seemed to be full of people and she hesitated in the doorway. Before she could give in to the cowardly impulse to retreat, Cole saw her.

''Addie!'' He came forward, grinning. ''I was starting to think you'd fallen asleep on us.''

''No. I'm too hungry to do that,'' she admitted.

''Me, too.'' He caught her hand and pulled her forward.

''You already ate half a pig while you were on the phone,'' Keefe commented.

"A small ham sandwich," Cole protested. "An appetizer."

"An appetizer for King Kong, maybe," Keefe said dryly. He looked at Addie and smiled. "How are you feeling?"

"I little bit like Alice after she fell down the rabbit hole," she replied. Looking at him, she could definitely understand why his word would be all the reassurance his niece would need. At first glance, he and Cole didn't look much alike. Keefe was a little taller than his youngest brother, his build bulkier. His hair was dark where Cole's was fair, and his smile was slower. But there was something in the angle of his jaw, in the steady confidence in his dark eyes, that made their relationship obvious. They were both men you could believe in.

She looked away from him as another tall man came forward. "I'm Kel Bryan. We met outside."

"I remember." It would be hard to forget a man of his striking good looks—dark hair and clear green eyes, a thick dark mustache and a killer smile tended to stick in a woman's mind, even when she was half-dazed by the rapid speed with which life had changed. "I wanted to thank you for everything you've done. Mr. Blackhawk said he worked for you."

"Lije works for me, but he volunteered to do the flying. The chopper belongs to one of my neighbors who was more than happy to loan it." His smile was quick. "I didn't do much. I'm just glad the two of you are okay."

"I was hoping to get a chance to thank Mr. Blackhawk again," Addie said.

"You can try." Kel shrugged. "Lije is about as talkative as a fence post though, so you won't get much out of him."

"Everybody find a seat," Megan said as she came into the room through the swinging door on the wall opposite where Addie had entered. "Supper's ready."

Addie didn't participate much in the conversation, especially not at first. She was too busy savoring the taste of real food—fried chicken, mashed potatoes and gravy, biscuits and three kinds of vegetables. She couldn't remember ever eating a meal that tasted even half as good. She let the conversation flow around her and concentrated on her food.

"I imagine Megan could come up with a can of sardines, if you'd like," Cole said after a little while.

He was sitting next to her and Addie glanced at him, her eyes smiling even though her mouth remained prim. "I don't think so."

"Might make you feel more at home," he insisted, his mouth curving in a teasing smile.

"Why do I have the feeling that we're missing something?" Kel said. "Are you particularly fond of sardines, Addie?"

The question made Cole laugh. Addie blushed a little but she smiled, too, and shook her head. "I hope I never see another sardine in my life."

It was left to Cole to tell the story of her purse full of emergency supplies. There was some laughter and a quick exchange of ideas on what you should carry to sustain you through a plane crash. All of the suggestions were silly and some bordered on the downright ludicrous. It was left to Kel and Megan's seven-year-old son to end the conversation.

"I'd pack a parachute and a telephone so I could jump out of the plane and then call for help," he announced in a tone that suggested he had serious doubts about the intelligence of the adults around him.

There was a moment of silence. "Out of the mouths of babes," Megan murmured with a grin.

"That's a very good idea, Michael," Kel told his son. "If I'm ever stranded in the wilderness, I'd want you with me for sure."

"Did you try calling your father again, Addie?" Megan looked across the table at her, her expression concerned.

"No. I'd just get the answering machine again." When they'd first arrived, Cole had insisted that Addie use the phone first. She'd called but had heard only her own voice—mechanical and a little nervous—as she suggested that the caller leave a message at the tone. She'd left a message for her father, telling him that she was safe but she knew he wouldn't check the machine for a couple more hours. "He won't be leaving the office for a while. There's no phone in there so he won't even know anyone has called."

Megan's eyebrows went up in surprise. "With you missing, wouldn't he want to stay by a phone?"

Addie's laugh was self-conscious. It was difficult to explain her father to people who didn't know him. "Father keeps a very strict schedule when he's writing. Nothing short of a cataclysm would get him to break it."

There was a short little silence when she finished speaking. No one said anything but she realized what they were probably thinking. To most parents, a missing child *was* a cataclysm. She felt her cheeks warm and bit her lip against the urge to offer an explanation, an excuse. She didn't need to explain her father's actions to anyone, she told herself. If she saw nothing wrong with his behavior, that was all that mattered. She knew he cared for her. In his own fashion.

"Did my nose deceive me or did I smell apple pie?" Cole asked, giving Megan a hopeful look.

"Your nose was on target," she assured him as she pushed back from the table and went to get dessert. The awkward moment was glossed over and apparently forgotten.

Cole leaned toward Addie and said something that made her smile. Keefe's dark eyes went from his youngest brother to Addie's face. He'd watched the two of them throughout the meal, seeing the casual intimacy between them. It was probably an inevitable result of the experience they'd shared. Facing death with someone tended to create some pretty tight bonds, at least temporarily.

But this seemed to go deeper than that, Keefe thought, seeing the way Addie's eyes lingered on Cole when he turned to say something to Kel. He wondered if Cole realized that she was halfway to being in love with him. Then again, from the look in Cole's eyes when he looked at her, maybe the question should be, Did he know he was halfway to being in love with *her?*

* * *

Addie had grown up as the only child of a man more interested in peoples long dead than he could ever be in anyone currently among the living. Even her mother had not been a particularly demonstrative person. What strong emotions Eileen Smith had felt had been directed toward her husband, who'd accepted them but had never, to Addie's knowledge, reciprocated them. Nothing in her background had prepared her for the Walker family.

She and Cole had barely set foot in the small terminal at the Santa Barbara airport before the welcoming party made themselves known. A small, thin little girl with long, dark gold hair and big brown eyes flew across the floor.

"Daddy!"

"Mary!" Cole dropped his duffel bag and crouched to catch her, swinging her up into his arms and holding her as if he'd never let her go. The love in his eyes was so open that Addie looked away, feeling as if she was witnessing something very private.

But no one else seemed to feel that way. The rest of the family swept down on them, laughing and, in the case of an older woman who had to be Cole's mother, openly crying. Addie tried to step back out of the way but somehow Keefe was in the way and the next thing she knew, she was caught up in the happy group. Nikki caught her in a tight hug.

"We were so worried," Nikki said. She stepped back and looked at Addie, her green eyes bright with tears. "I'm so glad you're all right."

"You think *you're* glad." Addie's laugh was shaky. She was touched by Nikki's obvious concern. Though the two of them had been close when they were in school, they hadn't seen much of each other lately.

"Addie, it's good to see you."

"Hello, Sam."

Nikki's husband took the hand she offered but used it to pull her forward for a quick, hard hug. Though she'd met Sam a couple of times and had liked him, she was surprised by the warmth of his welcome. But when she stepped back from his embrace, she found herself being hugged next by a tall, dark-haired knee-weakeningly gorgeous man who could only be Gage, and then his wife caught both of Addie's hands in hers.

"I'd hug you if I could get close enough," Kelsey Walker said, smiling at Addie, her eyes bright with happy tears. Her stomach, enormous with late pregnancy, made her meaning clear. "We're so glad you're all right. We've been so very worried about both of you."

And while Addie was still digesting the idea that perfect strangers had been concerned for her safety, Kelsey stepped aside and Addie was caught up in Rachel Walker's strong embrace. "Oh, my dear, we've all been worried sick. I'm so glad you're all right."

"Th-thank you," Addie stammered when Rachel released her. "I-it's very kind of you, Mrs. Walker."

"Kind?" Rachel seemed puzzled by Addie's choice of words. She smiled, her dark eyes warm and showing a hint of mischief that made her look very much like her youngest son. "Call me Rachel. I know we're going to be friends. There's something I've been dying to ask you, ever since talking to Cole this morning."

"What is it?"

"You have to tell me how you got Cole to eat sardines. He positively *hates* fish."

The laughter that followed served to release tension. And then everyone seemed to be talking at once, wanting to hear all about their "adventure," as Gage's young stepson called it. Addie felt as if she'd been swept up into the heart of a whirlwind. And "heart" was the operative word, she thought. The love the Walkers felt for one another was so open, so honest. She'd never seen anything like it, certainly not in her own family.

It was at least twenty minutes before it occurred to anyone that they were still standing in the middle of the airport. It was Gage who broke up the gathering.

"Kelsey's been on her feet long enough," he announced, sliding his arm around his wife.

"I'm okay," she protested, but she leaned a little into his support.

"Gage is right," Rachel said immediately. "You and my newest grandchild shouldn't be standing around on this hard floor."

"Why don't you all come back to our house?" Kelsey said, her smile including Addie. "I always cook when I'm worried, and these past few days I've cooked enough to feed a small army."

"She's not kidding," Gage said. "It's been like having the Tasmanian Devil in the kitchen, the way she'd been whirling around."

"He exaggerates a bit," Kelsey said dryly. She stroked one hand over the bulge of her stomach. "Trust me, I haven't whirled in at least four or five months."

There was a general move toward the door as everyone agreed that going to Gage and Kelsey's seemed like a good idea. Addie hung back, suddenly aware that, no matter how it had felt for the past few minutes, she was not a part of this family.

"Addie?" Cole stretched out his hand and caught hers in it. Mary, perched on his hip, regarded her with serious brown eyes that seemed much too old for a seven-year-old.

"I should go home." With Cole's fingers around hers, she was almost painfully aware that there was nothing she wanted to do more than go with him. She wanted desperately to extend the fantasy that she belonged just a little while longer. "My father will be anxious," she said.

There was an almost imperceptible moment of silence and she could almost read what everyone was thinking—if he was so anxious, why wasn't he here? She felt the color rise up from her throat to her face.

"He never drives in the city," she said, unaware of the slight, defiant lift of her chin.

"Of course," Rachel murmured, as if it didn't occur to her that, under the circumstances, he might have called a cab. "Sam, why don't you and Nikki drive Addie home and then join us at Gage and Kelsey's?"

"Oh, no. I can get a cab," Addie protested immediately. But she might as well have saved her breath because no one paid any attention to the suggestion.

"You're not going to let Keefe eat all the food before I get there, are you?" Sam demanded suspiciously.

"Trust me, there's more than enough to go around," Gage said dryly. "Kelsey's cooked enough to feed half the state."

"Besides, I'm not the one with the hollow leg in this family," Keefe said, giving his older brother a pointed look.

Addie barely heard the lighthearted argument that ensued. Cole had taken a half step away from the others, pulling her with him. "I'll call you," he said.

"Okay." She would have given a year of her life to be able to interpret the look in his eyes. There was an urgency there that seemed— She wasn't even going to let herself think about it. Because it would be too easy to fool herself into believing it was something it wasn't. And then her heart might be completely broken, rather than merely cracked.

"What kind of a father is this guy?" Sam demanded as he backed the truck out of the driveway. "His daughter is missing for almost a week and he can't even be bothered to come to the airport to pick her up?"

"I only met him a couple of times, but he struck me as being pretty cold." Nikki glanced one more time at the elegant brick facade of the house. Addie had turned to wave goodbye to them before letting herself into the house only moments before.

"Cold?" Sam put the truck in gear with more force than was strictly necessary. He stepped on the gas. "That's got to be putting it mildly. Did you see her face when she told us that he didn't like driving in traffic? Is there something wrong with taxis? Hell, the guy could have hired a limo. You can't tell me he can't afford it," he said, gesturing sharply to the expensive homes around them.

"He can afford it," Nikki agreed. "But from what Addie has told me, I don't think he spends much money except on his work. Archaeology doesn't come cheap."

"Neither do children," Sam snapped. "I can't even imagine how it feels to have a father like that."

"No, I don't suppose you can." Nikki reached out and patted his leg. "Not everyone comes from a family like yours, where everyone not only loves everyone else, they actually *like* each other."

"I know that." Sam caught her hand in his, squeezing it for a moment before releasing her. He knew Nikki's own family was far from the Brady Bunch image of perfection. But Ronald Smith's lack of concern over his daughter was something else again.

"I still say the guy's a jerk," he muttered, flipping on his turn signal.

"I agree. But Addie loves him. Or she thinks she does." Nikki frowned out the windshield, her expression thoughtful. "When we were in school, there was nothing she wanted more than his approval."

"Did she ever get it?"

"I don't know. I don't think it would have occurred to him to tell her if she had." Sam's response was a low, rumbling noise that sounded suspiciously like a growl. Nikki ignored him. She thought about the obvious intimacy between Cole and Addie. "She's spent so many years trying to get him to love her, I wonder if another man could ever compete."

"Father?" Addie stepped onto the cool tile of the foyer and shut the door behind her. Everything looked exactly the way it had when she'd left five days ago, but then, it had looked much the same for the twenty years before that.

The house and its furnishings had belonged to her paternal grandfather. She'd been seven when he died and her father had moved her and her mother into the big house. Aside from necessary repairs, everything had been left the way it was when her grandfather died. Eileen Smith's energies had been focused almost completely on her husband and seeing to his happiness, leaving precious little left over for her daughter and none at all for redecorating and updating the rather gloomy old house.

There had been times when Addie thought the house would have been the perfect funeral home, all dark paneling and heavy furniture, but the decor was the least of her concerns today.

"Father?"

"No need to shout, Adelaide. I heard you the first time." Ronald Smith came out of his study and walked toward his daughter. Looking at him, Addie felt the same sense of awe she'd felt in his presence when she was a child. It just didn't seem possible that this tall, elegant man could be her father. With his patrician features, thick, dark hair and crystal-clear blue eyes, he looked more like an aristocrat than an archaeologist. But, of course, he wasn't just *an* archeologist, he was one of the leaders in his field, a man whose brilliance and persistence had won him as many enemies as it had admirers.

"I'm home," she said, feeling suddenly very young and insignificant.

"So I see." One dark brow lifted in silent commentary on the foolishness of stating the obvious, and Addie flushed. "You look well."

"I'm fine. No injuries, aside from a slightly twisted ankle."

"I'm glad to hear it." He bent to brush a kiss across her forehead. It was an unusually demonstrative gesture for him and Addie felt guilty for thinking about the exuberance with which the Walkers had expressed themselves. It wasn't fair to compare the two. "I received the message saying you'd been found. I was quite relieved."

"I'm sorry you were worried," she said, smiling up at him.

"I was concerned," he corrected her. "Worry is a waste of time."

"Of course."

"I'm very glad that you're safe." He frowned a little. "It is a pity about Professor Upsinskia's library, of course. I had hoped to be able to start looking over some of the materials by now."

Addie swallowed the urge to apologize for getting involved in a plane crash when she should have been supervising the shipment of his colleague's library.

He sighed and lifted his shoulders, as if to say that what could not be cured must be endured. "I'll make other arrangements. I would have preferred to have someone supervise the shipment, of course, but that can't be helped."

Addie wondered if he was hinting that she might like to get back on a plane and fly to South Dakota to finish the task she'd started out to do. But she dismissed the thought. Her father didn't hint. If he'd wanted her to go to South Dakota, he wouldn't have hesitated to ask.

And a week ago she'd have filled her purse with food, swallowed her fear and gotten on a plane. But not now. Things were different now. *She* was different now. Cole had said he was going to call and, while she had no intention of sitting by the phone like a lovelorn teenager, neither did she plan on going out of town. Because if he called, she wanted to hear whatever he had to say.

Chapter 7

Cole listened to the phone ring and tried to decide what he should say to Addie when she answered. It was stupid to feel nervous. It wasn't like she was going to have forgotten who he was over the last week. But he was still as nervous as a boy about to ask a girl for a date for the very first time.

"Hello?" The voice was deep and masculine.

Cole had been so focused on what he was going to say to Addie that he was momentarily thrown off balance. Of course, since she lived with her father, he should have been prepared for the man to answer the phone.

"This is Cole Walker," he said, feeling more like a teenage boy by the minute. "Is Addie available?" In his mind, he heard the echo of a boy's voice—*Can I talk to your daughter, Mr. Smith?*

"Certainly," Ronald Smith said after an almost imperceptible pause. "Just a moment."

Cole had the distinct impression that the other man was less than delighted to hear from him. He wondered why. Not that he cared a whole hell of a lot what Ronald Smith thought, sight unseen. When the man hadn't bothered to meet Addie at the airport, Cole had taken an instant dislike to him. What kind of a father was he, anyway?

"Cole?" Addie's voice was soft and a little breathless, as if she'd hurried to the phone.

"Don't sound so surprised," he said teasingly. "I told you I'd call."

"Yes, but I didn't know if you'd meant it," she admitted with an honesty that made him think of his daughter. Like Mary, Addie hadn't learned to play games. It was a rare quality in anyone over the age of ten. And one of the things he liked most about her. He relaxed back into his desk chair and grinned at the phone.

"You should trust me," he chided her. "I would have called sooner but I've been up to my elbows in paperwork, dealing with the insurance companies and trying to figure out how I'm going to replace my plane."

"Can't you buy a new one?"

"Not one like that. Beech Craft quit making the D-18 a couple of decades ago. I've got feelers out for another one, though. That plane was older than I am." His voice was momentarily bleak as he considered what he'd lost.

"I'm sorry," Addie said softly.

"Thanks." Cole pushed aside the depressing thoughts. He could worry about the plane and what its loss was doing to his business another time. "But I didn't call to talk about that. I called to ask you out on a picnic."

"A picnic?"

"I know you're probably sick of dining alfresco at the moment. We did enough of it to last for a while."

"I'm not sure you could call a can of sardines and stale crackers 'dining alfresco,'" she said. Cole could hear the smile in her voice and felt his mouth curve in response.

"Maybe not. Actually, I've had my fill of nature for a while but it's great kite-flying weather and I promised Mary we'd take a picnic lunch to the park to see if we can get a kite caught in a tree."

"I thought the idea was to keep them *out* of the trees."

"Hush. I've spent years convincing my daughter that all the best kite flyers deposit their kites in trees on a regular basis."

Addie laughed. "I wouldn't dream of disabusing her."

Her laugh was another thing he liked about her. He'd missed hearing it this past week. In fact, he'd missed damn near everything about her. Cole grinned at the Ansel Adams calendar on the wall across from his desk. The cramped little office from which he ran his business—when he had a business to run—suddenly seemed a bit brighter.

"Good. I was afraid I was going to have to withdraw my invitation, which you haven't accepted yet, by the way."

"Wouldn't you and your daughter rather have some time alone?" she asked hesitantly.

"We've had a whole week alone. I think Mary's sick of me. Besides, she's curious about you. I think she'd like to meet the woman who was marooned with her father. The two of you can compare notes on how difficult I am to live with. It's short notice, I know, but kite-flying weather can't be predicted."

"That's okay. I didn't have anything planned."

"Then you'll join us?" He hadn't realized how much he'd wanted her to say yes until this moment.

"I'd love to."

They agreed on a time for him to pick her up, Cole assured her that she didn't need to bring anything but herself, and Addie hung up the phone, feeling as giddy as a girl about to go on her first date. Which, come to think of it, wasn't all that far from the truth, she thought, staring at the painfully serene painting of a mythical lake hanging above the old-fashioned gossip table that housed the phone in solitary splendor.

Attending an all girls school had tended to make dating difficult, to say the least. Of course, there had been Duane in college but she wasn't sure they'd ever actually dated. They'd just sort of... drifted together without fanfare. And their parting a few months later had been just as dull.

She was smiling as she turned away from the phone. Her smile widened when she saw her father standing in the doorway of his office.

"That was Cole," she said, her eyes sparkling with pleasure.

"So he said." He arched his brows in question. "I gather you're going out with him today?"

"On a picnic with him and his little girl." Addie was surprised and pleased by his interest. Ordinarily, she would have expected him to have dismissed the call from his thoughts as soon as he'd handed the phone to her.

He frowned slightly. "I'm a little surprised that you'd wish to see him again. I would have thought that, given what happened, you'd prefer to put the entire unpleasant incident behind you."

"It wasn't Cole's fault that we had to make a forced landing," she said, coming to his defense immediately. "Mechanical failures happen to even the most careful of pilots."

"Yes. Of course."

"And it wasn't *all* unpleasant," Addie continued, ignoring the wealth of doubt in his response. "Cole did his best to look after me. If it hadn't been for him, I'd still be stuck on that ledge. He saved my life, then."

"Of course." His long, elegant fingers tightened over the book he was holding. He smiled. "It's unlikely that I'd forget that."

She had the feeling that there was more he might have said, but for once in her life, she was less concerned with her father's feelings than she was with her own. If he had more to say, it was just going to have to wait. Cole was picking her up in less than an hour and she didn't want anything to spoil her anticipation.

"I don't know exactly when I'll be home," she said, moving toward the stairs. "I'll tell Mrs. Hodges that I might not be in for dinner."

"Have a good time on your picnic," he said.

"I will." Her smile and the excitement in her eyes revealed more than she realized. "I'll see you later."

She hurried up the stairs, unaware of her father's gaze following her, his expression thoughtful.

"You've really never flew a kite before?" Mary looked at Addie, her brown eyes, so like her father's, wide with disbelief.

"She's never *flown* a kite before," Cole corrected automatically as he lifted the kite from the back of his five-year-old Chevy Blazer.

"That's what I said," Mary said, looking surprised that her father hadn't heard her.

"You said 'flew.' You should have said 'flown.'" Cole found the ball of twine and shut the Blazer door.

"How come?" Mary looked up at him. The questioning tilt of her head put Addie in mind of a little bird.

"It has to do with using the proper tense," Cole explained. "Take my hand while we cross the street."

She took his hand obediently but she wasn't through exploring the differences between *flew* and *flown*. "What's a tense?" she asked as the three of them crossed the street.

"It's..." Cole stopped as it suddenly occurred to him that he was grossly ill-equipped to explain grammar to a seven-year-old. He threw a pleading look in Addie's direction. She grinned but waded in.

"It has to do with whether you're talking about something that happened in the past or something that's happening right now. 'I run' is present tense. 'I ran' is past tense."

"Oh." Mary appeared to consider this. Addie was just congratulating herself on passing a difficult test when the little girl spoke up again. "Is 'flew' in the past?"

"Yes, it is," Addie said, pleased by this evidence of her teaching skills.

"What about 'flown'? Is that a past thing?" Mary pursued, with the ruthlessness of the very young.

"Y-yes." Addie's answer was less prompt as she saw the jaws of the trap yawning wide at her feet.

"Then how come Daddy said one was right and the other wasn't?" Mary pounced in triumph on this evidence of the ultimate fallibility of adult logic.

"Well, it's because that's one of the rules of English."

"But how come?"

"The eternal cry of childhood," Cole said in response to the pleading look Addie sent him. "How come you always ask how come?" he asked his daughter, mock stern.

"'Cause how else am I supposed to learn stuff?" Mary said unanswerably.

Cole grinned. "I see a future for you in debating, urchin." He looked at Addie, his eyes full of pride and a rueful amusement. "You've got both of us on the ropes and we're going to have to fall back on the most annoying answer of all. 'Flown' is right and 'flew' is wrong because that's the way it is. There's probably a rule that explains it but I don't know what it is. Now, do you want to fly this kite or do you want an English lesson?''

Mary, not unexpectedly, chose kite flying over grammar. Her companions breathed a sigh of relief.

"I can't remember the last time I've had so much fun,'' Addie said late in the afternoon.

"I'm glad you enjoyed witnessing my humiliation.'' Cole leaned back on his elbows on the old army blanket they'd spread out for their picnic. He kept one eye on his daughter, who was playing nearby with some other children.

"I don't think you have to feel humiliated,'' Addie said soothingly. "They were very nice young men.''

"Ha! How would you feel if you were trying to impress your date, not to mention your only child, with your kite-flying prowess and managed to get the stupid thing caught in a tree first thing?''

Addie took a moment to enjoy hearing herself referred to as his "date" before attempting to reassure him. "It could have happened to anyone. You just didn't see the tree.''

"A sycamore half the size of Rhode Island is kind of hard to miss,'' Cole said disgustedly. "It was bad enough to get the kite hung up in it, but then to have a bunch of half-naked college kids offer to get it down for me...'' He shook his head as words failed him.

"They really were very nice," Addie said, biting her lip against a smile. "And I don't think it's fair to call them half-naked. They just weren't wearing shirts."

"It's January," Cole said. "What kind of a person goes without a shirt in January?"

"It's seventy-five degrees out."

"Yeah, but it's January," he said plaintively.

"I don't think there's a law against going without a shirt in January."

"There ought to be." Particularly for young men who looked as if they spent more time in the gym than they did in the classroom. At thirty-three, Cole thought he was a long way from being over the hill, but there was something about all those hard nineteen- and twenty-year-old bodies that had made him suck in his stomach and wonder if maybe he shouldn't start hitting the gym more often.

"They seemed like nice kids," Addie said. "And they didn't have to offer to let Mary fly their kite."

Cole snorted. "Just another attempt to make me look like an idiot," he grumbled.

"I think it was just because they liked Mary."

"She can be pretty hard to resist," he said. His eyes followed his daughter as she played tag with some other children. He watched, as always, for signs that she was getting overly tired.

"She's a very sweet little girl," Addie said, watching his face as he looked at Mary. It was so obvious that, as far as he was concerned, the sun rose and set in his little girl. "It must be difficult for you. Raising her alone, I mean."

"Raising a kid is never easy," Cole said. "Having a partner doesn't necessarily make it easier. My father died when I was eight and my mother was scared to death of trying to raise four boys on her own. She remarried a year or so after Dad's death, as much to provide us with a father as for anything else. The guy was a Class-A bastard."

He stared past her at things only he could see, his eyes dark with unhappy memories. His expression was bleak and Addie found herself reaching out to touch his hand, wanting both to offer comfort and to draw him back into the present. At her touch, Cole seemed to shake himself a little. He turned his hand, his fingers closing over hers.

"It was a long time ago," he said. "We came through it. More or less." His smile held a bittersweet edge and his fingers tightened over hers for a moment. "If there was anything good that came of it, it was that I learned that families come in all shapes. My mom did a pretty good job of being mother and father to the four of us." His smile widened and grew reminiscent. "Of course, she had help from Sam, who took it on himself to try and be the man of the family."

"He couldn't have been very old," Addie said.

"He'd just turned thirteen."

"That's a little young to be taking on that kind of responsibility."

"That's what Gage and Keefe and I thought. Especially Gage and me. We did our best to make his life a living hell." He said it with such simple pride that Addie laughed out loud.

"Poor Sam. He has my sympathies."

"He could've used them back then. It's a wonder he didn't throttle the two of us and bury us in the basement. I suspect a judge would have ruled it justifiable homicide."

She laughed again. "You must have been hellions."

"We weren't exactly angels," he said, making it clear that this was something of an understatement.

"You seem to be close to your brothers now, so you must have had at least a few redeeming virtues."

"We were always close. Even when we were fighting like cats and dogs amongst ourselves, we'd band together in an instant against any outside threat. Much as I resented Sam—and I resented him like hell at times—I always knew he'd be there for me if I needed him. We're family," he said, as if that explained everything.

"It sounds nice," Addie said wistfully.

"It is. Not that I appreciated it when I was a kid. I wanted to be Marlon Brando and it was damned hard to play the part of the lone rebel with three older brothers poised to drag me out of trouble." His grin held a reminiscent edge.

"I can see where that might have made things difficult," Addie agreed. Though her expression remained appropriately solemn, there was a suspicious tuck in her cheek. Cole gave her a mock scowl.

"You can laugh, but it was tough. I worked my butt off the summer after I turned sixteen so I could make enough money to buy a motorcycle and a black leather jacket. I practiced looking world-weary and learned to slouch. I even took up smoking, but that didn't last long."

"What happened?" she asked.

"My mother said she couldn't stop me from killing myself on a motorcycle but she wasn't going to tolerate me getting lung cancer and stinking up the house in the process."

"I would think that was just the challenge a budding rebel would be looking for. Full-blown parental suppression, proof that the older generation doesn't understand your angst."

Cole grinned but shook his head. "You don't know my mother. She never had to raise a hand to any of us. All she had to do was give us this 'look' and we'd all leap to do whatever she wanted."

"Just a look?"

"That's all it took." He shook his head, his eyes following Mary as she played with the other children. "I've never figured out how she did it but there was just something about it that made you willing to do anything just to see her smile at you again. Maybe it had something to do with Dad being gone. I guess it made us all feel a little protective of her. Anyway, it made it a lot harder to be a proper renegade when I couldn't smoke. I mean, what's a renegade without a cigarette dangling from the corner of his mouth?"

"It does seem a necessary prop," Addie agreed, her sympathy somewhat diluted by the laughter that danced in her eyes.

"Yeah. I thought I could redeem myself if I got in trouble with the law, but my heart wasn't really in it."

"I suppose even the best of rebels might be discouraged by the prospect of tangling with the police."

"It wasn't the police that scared me. A little legal persecution was just what I wanted. A few hot lights and rubber hoses would have added an authentic edge to my world-weariness. It was the thought of Mom giving me one of her 'looks' that kept me from robbing a liquor store. That and the fact that Sam was at the police academy by then and I figured it wouldn't do his career much good to have a brother in jail."

"A thoughtful rebel," Addie said on a giggle. "I think that's an oxymoron."

"I suppose it is. If only I'd been lucky enough to have been born an orphan, I could have given Brando a run for his money," he said wistfully.

Addie laughed, entranced by the image of him as a would-be rebel of sixteen, finding himself balked at every turn by his close relationship with his family. She couldn't help but contrast that image with the distance she'd always felt from her own parents, the distance she still felt from her father.

But she didn't want to think about that today. Tilting her head back, she stared up into the winter bare branches of the kite-eating sycamore. The kite itself was propped against the base of the tree, its jaunty scarlet body somewhat the worse for wear. Aerial disasters or no, she couldn't remember the last time she'd had so much fun.

"So, what did you decide to do when you realized you couldn't be Marlon Brando?" she asked, turning her head to smile at Cole. His fingers felt warm and strong around hers and she wondered if he'd forgotten that he was still holding her hand.

"After high school, I moved to L.A. and spent some time working as a stuntman."

"Really? What movies were you in?"

"Nothing you're likely to have seen."

"How do you know? Nikki and I used to go to the movies fairly often when I lived in Burbank."

"Then you definitely wouldn't have seen anything I made. I don't think any of the films I worked on were in the theaters for more than ten or fifteen minutes at the most. Most of them went straight to video and I think a couple of them bypassed video and showed up immediately on the late, late, late show. The only people who ever saw them were insomniac couch potatoes with no taste."

"They couldn't have been that bad," she protested.

"They were worse." He pulled his face into a comical grimace. "After Sam saw one of them, he told me I should be grateful that they'd left the *k* out of Walker so no one ever had to know I'd been connected with it."

"Cole Waler?" Addie giggled. "What kind of a movie was it?"

"It's a little hard to describe." Cole frowned as he considered her question. "It was sort of a martial arts, mystery, gore fest with a lot of sex thrown in. I never did figure out what it was about. I just know I spent a lot of time getting kicked in the stomach by the hero who, if I remember correctly, turned out to be a vampire at the end of the movie."

"It certainly sounds...interesting," she said after a moment.

"It was awful," Cole said absently. He released her hand and sat up abruptly, his eyes scanning the slope below. "Do you see Mary?"

"She's right over there." Addie pointed to the left.

Mary's bright pink T-shirt was plainly visible in the midst of a group of four or five children. They were standing next to a huge hound of uncertain parentage who was patiently shaking hands with each of them.

"Looks like she's made a new friend," Addie commented as Mary shook the dog's paw for the second time. She admired Cole's parental vigilance but she missed the feel of him holding her hand. It had been pleasant, even if he hadn't known he was doing it.

"Poor dog." Cole relaxed, his mouth curving in a smile as he watched his daughter. "She's going to bug me to get her a dog again. She's been asking for one for the last year. My mother has a dog the size of a small pony. Every time Mary spends the night with Grandma, I get to hear about all the neat things Hippo did."

"Hippo? The dog's name is Hippo?" Addie's eyebrows rose.

"Mary's idea. When he yawns, he looks like he could swallow a whole boatload of tourists with ease. If he had a brain, he might be dangerous, but he's the dumbest animal I've ever seen. Year before last, he stole the half-cooked Thanksgiving turkey off the counter. We ate hamburgers and chicken that year."

"He sounds...interesting. I can see why he'd inspire a seven-year-old with a desire for a dog of her own."

"Yeah. I guess I'll have to break down and get her one." He frowned as he said it.

"You don't look enthused. Don't you like dogs?"

"It's not that. Puppies demand a lot of energy. I worry about her overdoing it." He caught the look of surprise Addie threw him and he lifted one shoulder in a half shrug. "Mary has a heart condition. The common term is a hole in the heart. She's not supposed to exert herself too much."

"Is she..." Addie looked at Mary, laughing in the sunlight, and felt a sharp pain in her chest at the thought of anything being wrong with the bright, loving little girl. "I don't know anything about the condition," she said.

"She'll be all right." Cole answered the question she hadn't been able to find the words to ask. "They can do surgery to repair the problem, but they want to wait until she's a little older, until her heart is bigger."

"But once they do the surgery, she will be okay?" Addie was surprised by the strength of her own concern. She'd only known Mary a few hours, but there was a sweetness about her, a charm that made it difficult to think of anything happening to her.

"She should be. They tell me the surgery is fairly routine these days, as routine as any surgery gets, I guess."

"I'm glad," she said simply.

"Me, too."

Before either of them could say anything more, Mary's voice reached them, demanding that they both come and meet Bill. From her gestures, it was apparent that Bill was the name of her new canine friend.

"Bill?" Cole said, arching one dark brow. "What kind of a name is that for a dog?" He stood and stretched his hand down to her.

"Some people might say the same about 'Hippo,'" Addie stated. She took his hand and let him pull her to her feet.

"Not after they've met the beast," he assured her. "One glimpse of Hippo and the only thing anyone is likely to wonder is why we didn't name him Elephant."

"Too much of a mouthful."

Addie started to pull her hand from his, only to have his fingers tighten around hers. She looked up at him in surprise. His eyes were warm with an emotion she couldn't name. Or maybe it was that she was afraid to name it, for fear she might be wrong. And *that* she couldn't bear.

Her color a little higher than normal, she allowed her hand to remain in his as they walked down the slope to where Mary waited for them.

Cole parked the truck at the curb and turned off the engine. In the back seat, Mary was asleep, her head resting against the window.

"I had a wonderful time," Addie said, pitching her voice just above a whisper to avoid waking the sleeping child. She unbuckled her seat belt and reached for the handle on her door.

"Wait." Cole got out of the truck and came around to her door, opening it for her and offering his hand as she stepped down onto the curb.

"Thank you." Addie flushed with pleasure at the old-fashioned courtesy.

"I suppose it's not politically correct to open a door for a woman these days," he said as he eased the door shut behind her.

"I can live with it. As long as you don't call me 'little lady' or 'doll.'"

"I'll keep that in mind."

Addie was vividly aware of the warm pressure of his fingers around hers as they walked up the brick pathway. By unspoken, mutual consent, they stopped just outside the yellow-tinted circle of light cast by the graceful brass lantern that lit the porch. Cole turned toward her and Addie felt her pulse skip a little.

"I had a wonderful time," she repeated, focusing her gaze on the wedge of skin made visible by the open neck of his shirt.

"You said that once." Cole tightened his fingers around hers, pulling her half a step closer. His other hand came up, his fingertips brushing a wisp of silky brown hair back from her forehead.

"I just wanted you to know," Addie said, her heart suddenly thumping against her breastbone.

"Know what?" Cole's breath was warm against her forehead.

"That... that I had a wonderful time," she whispered breathlessly.

"Good." He smoothed his hand against her head, his palm cupping her cheek, his thumb under her chin, tilting her face up to his. "May I?"

Addie had been staring, mesmerized, at his mouth, but the husky question brought her eyes up to his. "May you what?"

"Kiss you?" he asked, his mouth a whisper away from hers.

There was something strangely erotic about the question. Addie felt her knees weaken. Her right hand was still caught in his but her left came up to rest against his chest, feeling the solid beat of his heart beneath her palm.

"May I kiss you?" he asked again, so close that she could almost taste him.

"Yes, please," she whispered, polite as a child who'd just been asked if she'd like another piece of candy. She felt rather than saw Cole's quick smile and then his mouth closed over hers and the world shivered around her.

She hadn't forgotten the other times he'd kissed her—once in anger, once in comfort. In the days since their rescue, she'd pulled the memories out more times than she could remember. She'd half convinced herself that what she'd felt then had been the product of circumstances—their isolation, the danger and uncertainty of their situation. But it hadn't been any of those things.

Standing here, in the soft, cool darkness, the safety of her own home only a few feet away, Addie felt her bones dissolve, felt the world fade away until Cole seemed the only solid thing in the universe. With a sigh, she opened her mouth to him, feeling his tongue slide into the sweet warmth she offered. The shiver that ran up her spine was one of pure awareness.

It was not a long kiss but what it lacked in length, it more than made up for in impact. When Cole lifted his mouth from hers, Addie's breathing was ragged and her knees were weak. It took a considerable effort of will to lift her lashes and look up into his face.

"I want to see you again." In the small portion of her brain that was still functional, she was aware that his breathing was none too steady, either—aware of it and pleased by this evidence that she wasn't the only one affected by the embrace.

"Okay." It was all she was capable of at the moment.

"Tomorrow?" he asked.

"Okay."

"I'll call you."

"Okay."

He grinned, his teeth gleaming in the darkness. "Is that all you can say?"

"Yes," she said simply, beyond coming up with a more clever response.

His chuckle was warm. He dropped a quick, hard kiss on her mouth. "You'd better get inside before you find yourself agreeing to something you're not ready for."

I'm ready, she wanted to tell him. She'd never been more ready in her life, but she could hardly say as much. Even if she'd had the courage, this was not the time or place to throw herself at his feet, not with his daughter asleep in the truck and the two of them standing only a few feet from her father's house. She didn't say anything but perhaps he read something of what she was feeling in her eyes. With a smothered groan, he bent to cover her mouth with his again.

When he released her moments later, Addie was nearly sure that her knees had dissolved. It seemed a miracle that they still supported her. Feeling a little wobbly, she moved obediently when Cole put his hands on her shoulders and turned her toward the porch.

"I'll call you tomorrow," he said again when she reached the top of the stairs.

Addie nodded without turning to look at him. If she looked at him again, she just might forget all about things like pride and dignity and throw herself into his arms. She stepped into the house and leaned back against the door, listening to the sound of the truck engine as it pulled away from the curb. She was still standing there when it faded into the distance, her mouth curved in a foolish little smile, her eyes dreamy.

She was unaware of her father standing in the doorway to his study, watching her, his blue eyes thoughtful and not particularly happy.

Chapter 8

As it happened, Addie didn't see Cole for almost a week. The day after their picnic, he got a call from a friend in Seattle who knew of a plane that he thought might be a suitable replacement for the one lost in the mountains.

"A friend of mine has been letting me use one of his planes to keep Walker Air running, but I can't keep that up forever," he explained over the phone. "The plane Bob found sounds like a pretty good possibility. It needs a little work—mostly cosmetic stuff—but the price is right. If it works out, I could fly it back from Seattle and be back in business in a week."

"That would be great," Addie said sincerely. Though he hadn't said much, she knew that he'd been worried about finding another plane. Owning a business of your own might be one of the great American dreams but it didn't leave much margin for error.

"I'll call you when I get back," he said.

"I'd like that."

They spoke a few minutes longer before saying goodbye. Addie turned away from the phone and wandered over to the French doors that led out onto the patio. The weather had shifted overnight and yesterday's sunshine had disappeared behind a thick ceiling of gray clouds and a light, drizzly rain was falling. The intricate herringbone pattern of the brick patio floor gleamed deep red from the moisture and the immaculately kept gardens beyond seemed almost painfully lush and green. The view was exquisite, worthy of a full color spread in a garden magazine.

Addie stared at it unseeingly. She was disappointed that she wasn't going to see Cole for a few days. But she was also a little relieved. She needed time to gather her thoughts, time to try to sort out her feelings. Last night, when he'd kissed her... She felt her face warm just thinking about it. It had been like being swept up in a whirlwind.

She'd always thought of herself as rather cool, not a woman given to strong passions. When her relationship with Duane had turned out to be less than thrilling, she'd assumed that the fault was a good part hers. She just wasn't a sexually exciting—or excitable—woman. Obviously, that wasn't quite true. If Mary hadn't been with them, if Cole had asked her to go home with him last night, she would have gone in a minute.

Staring out at the rain-soaked gardens, she wondered how it was possible that she could know herself so little. A few weeks ago she would have said that she wasn't particularly interested in having a serious relationship with a man. Her work as her father's assistant was interesting. There were moments when she almost believed that working together was drawing them closer, that they might finally achieve a measure of the closeness she'd dreamed about since she was a child.

If she occasionally looked ahead a few years and worried a little about the direction her life was going, she was generally able to shove those worries out of sight. She was only twenty-seven. Her biological clock might be ticking but it wasn't exactly tolling a warning bell. There was plenty of time to think about having a child, if she decided she wanted one. Besides, to have children, one needed a man and she was more than half convinced that she had little to offer any man by way of passion.

Her reaction to Cole had certainly proven her wrong on that one, she thought with a sigh. But it wasn't so much her physical response to him that concerned her. He was an attractive man, after all. What worried her was the knowledge that what she felt for Cole Walker went a great deal deeper than plain old lust. What scared her to death was the thought that she was more than halfway to falling in love with the man.

Her eyes followed the meandering pattern made by a raindrop as it slid across the glass of the door. She couldn't imagine anything more lonely than to be in love alone. Addie brushed her fingertips impatiently across the dampness on her lashes. If she'd really done something as foolish as falling in love with Cole, then it would be better to save the tears for when her heart broke, because it was sure to happen.

She sniffed as she turned away from the damp, gray weather outside. It was a very good thing that Cole had gone away for a little while. With luck, he'd get his plane and she'd get a chance to get hold of her emotions before they slipped completely out of her control.

"Looking for someone?" Gage's question came from behind Cole and he turned to look at his older brother.

"I should have gone to pick Addie up," he said by way of an answer. "Friday night traffic was miserable."

"You're worse than a hen with one chick," Gage said, his clear blue eyes sparkling with amusement. "She's not even fifteen minutes late. I don't think you'd worry this much about Mary."

"Mary's not old enough to drive," Cole said, but his grin was a rueful acknowledgment that he might be overreacting. "I guess I got in the habit of worrying about Addie after the crash."

"Playing Swiss Family Robinson brought out the protective instincts, huh?"

"More or less." Cole glanced at the doorway again but it remained stubbornly empty. "She did say she was coming, right?"

Gage's grin widened but he answered seriously enough. "When Kelsey told her that we all wanted to get together and sort of celebrate the fact that the two of you had been returned to what passes for civilization these days, Addie said she would absolutely be here.''

The gathering was being held in one of Santa Barbara's trendiest restaurants. They'd been able to secure a private room on short notice because Kelsey's best friend was engaged to the chef/owner. The fact that Kelsey's organically grown vegetables provided the main ingredients for some of Anton's most popular dishes hadn't hurt, either. Glancing around at the room, which was done in shades of pink and gray, with exposed ducts and pipes giving it a vaguely industrial look, Cole could only hope that the food was more to his taste than the decor.

''Did Kelsey invite Addie's father?''

''He declined to attend. Something about having other plans for this evening.''

''I'm not surprised. I haven't met him yet but the guy sounds like a first-class bastard. Not that Addie has said as much.''

''Yeah, well, he didn't make a favorable impression on any of us when he didn't bother to show up at the airport,''Gage said.

''You must be talking about Addie's perennially absent parent,'' Sam said as he joined them. He gestured to the waiter who'd just entered the room. ''You guys want something to drink?''

''I'm driving,'' Gage said, shaking his head.

''And I'm flying in the morning.''

"Looks like I'm drinking alone then," Sam said. He caught the waiter's attention and ordered a Dos Equis. "You taking up the new plane?" he asked.

"No." Cole laughed. "I nursed it down here from Seattle but it needs some work before I take it up again. Joe says I can keep using his plane until I get mine in shape."

"Lucky for you he's got a spare plane lying around," Gage said.

"What he's got is more money than you can shake a stick at. He's got half a dozen planes sitting around."

"Ah, the idle rich." Gage shook his head in mock disapproval.

"Joe's about as idle as the Road Runner," Cole said. "He spends so much time making money, he doesn't have any left over for enjoying it. He spends so little time at home that he probably has to wear a name tag so his kids know who he is."

"Life's too short," Sam said as he took the glass of beer the waiter handed him.

"Amen to that," Cole said. There was nothing like surviving a plane crash to bring you to the full realization of just how short life could be. He changed the subject. "Gage says Keefe isn't coming."

"Too much work." Sam took a swallow of beer. "Jace picked up the slack while he was in Wyoming but it takes the two of them to keep the place running. Keefe didn't want to leave again so soon."

"How are things going?" Cole asked. "Are they going to break even this year?"

"I didn't ask and you know Keefe, he didn't say."

"He would have made a great spy," Gage said. "I've seen fence posts reveal more secrets."

"True." Sam frowned at his beer a moment before lifting his head to look at his brothers. "I have a feeling things aren't going too well."

"Ranching isn't exactly an easy way to make a living," Cole commented. "Sometimes I think it was bad luck that won him that poker hand and saddled him with The Flying Ace."

"Except it got him off the rodeo circuit," Gage acknowledged. "And at the rate he was going, he was bound to break his neck within a year."

"He's a damned good rider," Sam said quickly. Only a year apart in age, he and Keefe were particularly close.

"I didn't say he wasn't. But after he and Dana split up, he started taking chances he shouldn't have taken. You know it. I know it. Jace knew it and damned near got his teeth knocked out for telling Keefe that if he wanted to commit suicide, there were quicker and easier ways to do it. I happened to be in Santa Fe that night. Keefe was completely out of control. As far as I'm concerned, even if he loses the ranch and his shirt along with it, it served a purpose by giving him something else to do while he got over Dana."

"*If* he got over her," Cole muttered, thinking of his former sister-in-law. He'd never met a more beautiful woman. Tall, blond, with a long, lean body that should have looked boyish and was anything but, Dana Walker had turned heads and accelerated pulses wherever she went. Keefe had taken one look at her, fallen head over heels and pursued her with single-minded determination until she agreed to marry him. Cole had certainly been able to understand Keefe's attraction to her but he'd always found her a little cool and distant for his taste.

"He's over her." Sam said it firmly, making Cole wonder if he was speaking from knowledge or hope. But Keefe and his feelings for his ex-wife, if any, were forgotten when he looked over Sam's shoulder and saw Addie walking into the room.

"Excuse me," he said hastily, and moved toward her.

His brothers turned to watch him greet her, saw the quick smile that lit Addie's face, taking her from ordinary to softly pretty, saw the quick brush of Cole's fingers against her cheek, the subtle intimacy of the gesture.

"Think he knows how bad he's got it?" Gage asked.

"Nope." Sam took a swallow of his beer and considered his youngest brother. "Think he knows she's in love with him?"

"Nope."

"Think he knows he's in love with her?"

"Nope."

Addie would have given a great deal to be half as sure of Cole's feelings for her as his brothers were. She wasn't even completely sure of her feelings for him. Or at least, she wasn't ready to admit that she was more than halfway to being in love with him. It was too bad she couldn't think of any other explanation for the way her heartbeat accelerated every time she saw him.

She'd had six days to convince herself that what she felt was nothing more than physical attraction. And then he smiled at her and she felt something dissolve inside and knew she was lying to herself. Whatever she felt for Cole, it went much deeper than simple physical desire, dammit.

But this was neither the time nor the place to fall into an emotional funk. Besides, it was difficult to imagine a funk of any kind surviving dinner with the Walker family. There was too much talk and too much laughter for a bleak mood to stand a chance. And, while she might end up with a broken heart somewhere farther down the line, right here and now, she was thoroughly enjoying her view into the workings of a family so different from her own.

When she was a child, dinner conversation had generally consisted of her father talking about his work while she and her mother formed an appreciative audience. With the Walkers, it seemed as if everyone talked at once and on several different topics. It should have been chaotic but no one seemed to lose the thread of the various conversations.

She'd always been discouraged from talking "unless you have something worthwhile to say, Adelaide." Since she was never sure what was worthwhile and what wasn't, she'd opted for remaining silent more often than not. But no one here seemed in the least concerned with "worthwhile" conversation and Mary and Gage's son, Danny, were listened to with every bit as much interest as any of the adults.

Despite her internal turmoil, Addie realized that she was enjoying herself very much. Not least of all because Cole was sitting next to her, drawing her into the conversation, his hand touching her arm from time to time, his smile making her feel as if she belonged. Oh, yes, she was definitely headed for heartbreak.

"Are you enjoying being back in civilization?"

Grateful for the distraction, Addie turned to smile at Jason Drummond. The older man was seated to her left. He had been a friend of Nikki's grandfather and Addie had met him once or twice when she and Nikki were in school together. She'd been a little puzzled by his inclusion in what was essentially a Walker family gathering until she'd seen the way he looked at Rachel Walker—not to mention the way she looked at him. The affection between them was plain to see.

"Actually, I have slightly mixed feelings," Addie said in response to his question. "Civilization seems very noisy and way too crowded. But the thing I've really noticed is the plumbing."

"Plumbing?" His gray brows rose in question.

"I don't think I ever really appreciated it until now. I know there are people who say that civilization began when man learned to control fire or when he learned to shape tools, but frankly, I think true civilization wasn't achieved until the advent of indoor plumbing."

"That's an interesting theory," Sam said, speaking across the table. His blue eyes were bright with humor. "You don't think the invention of the written word might qualify as the start of civilization?"

"No." Addie shook her head, aware that the conversation had drawn the attention of the others at the table. She wasn't accustomed to finding herself the center of attention but there was nothing intimidating about their friendly interest. "Running water is an essential to civilization."

"Maybe you should write a paper on it," Gage suggested.

"Yes, but would she present it at a meeting of experts or a plumbers convention?" Nikki asked.

"The plumbers," Cole said. "Definitely the most appreciative audience for something like that."

The discussion that followed was completely frivolous but no one seemed to object. In fact, they all seemed to revel in taking the nonsense to even greater heights—or depths, depending on your point of view.

Addie was laughing at some comment of Sam's when she saw Kelsey set her hand on Gage's sleeve. He leaned toward her, tilting his head to hear what she was saying. Addie had thought Kelsey was looking a little pale all evening but it was nothing compared to the ashen tint that stole over Gage's face.

"You're what?" His appalled tone rose over the table, stopping conversation dead. All heads turned in his direction. Finding herself suddenly the cynosure of all eyes, Kelsey's face flushed. Gage's dazed eyes shifted from his wife to his family. "She's in labor."

"Why don't you take an ad on the ten o'clock news?" Kelsey suggested tartly.

"It's hardly the kind of thing you can keep secret, my dear," Rachel Walker said calmly. "How long have you been in labor?"

"It started this afternoon."

"This afternoon?" Gage's voice rose incredulously. "Why didn't you say something? What are you doing here? Why aren't we at the hospital?"

"Why don't you calm down," Sam suggested, reading the temper in Kelsey's eyes. He put his hand on his brother's arm. "Kelsey knows what she's doing."

"Thank you," Kelsey said, shooting a pointed look in her husband's direction.

"Sorry." Gage drew a deep breath and gave her a smile that couldn't completely conceal his nervousness. "I know you wouldn't do anything you shouldn't."

"What's wrong, Mama?" Danny left his seat and came around to stand by his mother's chair.

"Nothing's wrong," Gage said, his own nervousness forgotten in the need to reassure the boy. "Your mom says it's time for the baby to get here."

"Right here?" Danny looked doubtful about the idea of his new brother or sister arriving at the restaurant.

"At the hospital, sweetie," Kelsey said, smiling at her son. "You remember how I explained that Daddy and I would go to the hospital so I could have the baby, don't you?"

"Yeah." Now that the moment was here, Danny looked less than comfortable with the idea. "Can I come, too?"

"We're all going to the hospital," Rachel said. "Sam, why don't you drive Gage and Kelsey? Danny, you can come with Jason and me. Cole, you take care of things here and then you and Addie and Mary can meet us at the hospital.''

No general could have disposed of troops on a battlefield with greater efficiency. Rachel's brisk tone created order out of potential chaos. Everyone moved to obey. In less than ten minutes, the private dining room was emptied except for Addie and Mary, Cole having gone off to find Anton to tell him why no one was going to be ordering dessert.

"Is your grandma always so...efficient?" Addie asked, feeling a little dazed by the speed with which the party had been dispersed.

"She's real good at getting everyone to do stuff," Mary said. She sat on a chair, the folds of her robin's egg blue dress neatly arranged around her, her silky gold hair neatly caught back from her face with matching blue barrettes. She looked sweetly feminine.

Addie had a sudden memory of herself at that age. She'd never managed to stay tidy for more than five minutes at a time. No matter how hard she tried, there always seemed to be something—a ribbon untied or buttons done up crooked or a hem coming down. Not only had she been physically rumpled, she'd never had even a fraction of Mary's calm self-possession. She wondered if it was the little girl's illness that had given her that almost adult calm.

"I like your dress," Addie told her.

"Thank you. Aunt Nikki bought it for me. She says Daddy's taste is all in his mouth and that he shouldn't be allowed to buy clothes for anybody.''

Addie laughed. "That sounds like Nikki. When we were in school together, she used to refuse to go shopping with me unless I promised not to buy anything before she saw it. But I'm sure she didn't mean that your father had bad taste."

"Yes, she did. Daddy knows lots about other stuff but he's not so good with colors."

"So, the minute my back is turned, you start telling my deep dark secrets," Cole said as he came back into the room.

"It's not a secret," Mary told him.

"It's certainly not now," he said, giving her a mock scowl.

"Your secret's safe with me," Addie promised.

"But it's not a secret," Mary insisted.

"So what you're saying is that everyone knows I have no taste?" Cole asked, laughing. "I don't have to worry about getting an overgrown ego as long as you're around, urchin." He tugged her hair, smiling down at her with such open affection that Addie felt her heart twist a little. She'd have sold her soul to have seen that look in her father's eyes just once when she was growing up.

"I've got everything straightened out with Anton so we can join the family at the hospital. Why don't you come with us, Addie? I can bring you back later to get your car."

"I can't go with you," she protested.

"Of course you can." Cole looked surprised that she'd think otherwise.

"No, I can't." Addie shook her head. "This is something for family."

"And friends," Cole insisted stubbornly. "We want you there, don't we, Mary?"

Mary looked at Addie speculatively, her head tilted to one side as she considered her response. She had the clear, honest gaze of the very young and Addie felt as if she were being weighed and measured in some way she couldn't define.

"I'd like you to come," she said, giving Addie a smile of singular sweetness. "Daddy and me both want you to come."

"Then it's settled," Cole said briskly. "You're coming with us."

"My father will be expecting me home soon." But it was a weak protest and they all knew it.

"You can call him from the hospital," Cole said, sweeping her and Mary out the door.

"But I don't understand why you're at the hospital," her father said half an hour later.

Addie chewed on her lower lip and wondered how she was supposed to explain something to him that she didn't understand herself. Coming to the hospital had seemed almost inevitable when Cole and Mary had insisted that she belonged with the family. Now, with her father's puzzled voice in her ear, it seemed more peculiar than inevitable.

"Cole asked me to come," she said weakly. "The whole family is here."

"It's one thing for the family to be there. Though, frankly, I should think they'd be better served by going home and letting someone call them in the morning to give them any news."

"The Walkers are very close," Addie said, thinking the word was hopelessly inadequate when it came to explaining the ties that bound the family together.

"Perhaps they are, but that still doesn't explain why you're there," he said, sounding puzzled. "You're not part of their family."

No, but I'd give almost anything if I were. Addie was surprised by the strength of that thought. Closing her eyes, she leaned her forehead against the cool metal of the pay phone. It was stupid enough to have fallen in love with Cole, but now she was more than half in love with the whole family. Damn. Damn and double damn.

"Adelaide?" Her father's voice sounded small and distant in her ear. "Are you still there?"

"Yes, but I have to go. There's someone waiting to use the phone," she added, glancing over her shoulder at the empty corridor. "Obviously, I don't know how long it will be until Kelsey has her baby so don't worry about me if I'm not home before morning. Good night."

As it happened, Kelsey surprised everyone by giving birth after only three hours of labor. Shortly before midnight, Lily Marie Walker made her entrance into the world, announcing her arrival with a healthy wail and terrifying her father with her fragility.

Before collapsing into one of the waiting room chairs, Gage managed to announce that both mother and child were doing fine. "Never again," he muttered. "My nerves can't take it."

"Is Mama okay?" Danny asked, leaning against his stepfather's leg. He'd fallen asleep with his head on his grandmother's lap and his small face was flushed with sleep, his eyes wide and anxious.

"Your mom is doing great," Gage told him firmly. He scooped Danny up onto his lap and gave him a reassuring hug. "She said to tell you she loved you very much."

"Can I see her?"

"In the morning. You can see her and your new little sister both."

"I can't see Mama now?" Danny was not sure he was all that anxious to see this new little sister everyone seemed so enthused about. "Just to see she's okay?"

Gage hesitated a moment, reading the anxiety in the little boy's eyes. Danny's father, Gage's best friend, had been killed when Danny was little more than a baby. Although he barely remembered Rick, he knew what it was to lose a parent. Gage could tell him that Kelsey was okay but he needed to see for himself.

"Sure you can," he said, standing with the boy in his arms. "Let me see what I can manage."

"After you've seen your mother, why don't I come home with you and your dad," Rachel said. "And maybe Mary could come to?" She glanced at Cole questioningly. He nodded.

"Sure, if Mary wants to do a sleep-over, it's fine with me."

"How would that be?" Gage asked. "If your grandma Rachel and your cousin Mary spent the night with us?"

Danny nodded, looking a little less anxious. Everyone was behaving so normally that it was hard to believe anything could be terribly wrong. "Will you make teddy bear pancakes?" he asked Rachel.

"Absolutely."

"Sounds good to me," Gage said.

From the slightly gray tint of his skin, Addie doubted if food of any kind held much appeal for him. He looked as if he needed a stiff drink and a good night's sleep more than anything else. He and Danny went to visit Kelsey and there was a few minutes of confusion in the waiting room. Cars were sorted out, arrangements were made for everyone to have a place to sleep for the night and, without quite knowing how it happened, Addie found herself alone with Cole, sitting in his truck in the hospital parking lot.

"I don't think it's hit Gage yet," she commented as Cole slid behind the wheel. "That he's a father, I mean."

"I think right now, he's just relieved that Kelsey is okay. Tomorrow, it will hit him that he's got a brand-new baby on his hands."

Cole shut the door, closing them in together. He slid the key into the ignition but didn't turn it. "It's been a busy night."

"But a good one." Addie tugged the collar of her jacket closer around her throat. Tonight, for a little while, she'd finally realized what being part of a family could mean. The glimpse into another world had warmed her.

"Are you tired?"

"A little." Addie shot him a curious look, her attention caught by something in his tone. "How about you?"

"A little." He spoke absently, as if his thoughts were elsewhere.

"Once you drop me off at the restaurant, you can go home and get some sleep," she said.

He didn't say anything for a moment. Nor did he start the truck. Addie was about to ask if something was wrong when he turned to look at her. Even in the dimly lit cab of the truck, she could see the intensity in his expression.

"Come home with me."

He said it quietly, the words not quite a demand but more than a question. Addie stared at him, her heart suddenly beating in her throat. *Come home with me.* She knew what he was asking. He was asking her to sleep with him.

It wasn't a decision she could make lightly. She'd have to think about it. Certainly, she couldn't just go home with him tonight. He was suggesting that they become lovers and that deserved some thought, some discussion. They'd have to lay out the ground rules, understand the situation exactly, make sure they both knew what they were getting into. She'd have to—

"Yes," she heard herself saying. Caution, common sense and practicality were all thrown out the window with that single word. It was insane and she'd surely have regrets. But she'd worry about that later. Tonight she wasn't going to think of anything but the moment.

"Yes, I'll go home with you."

"Good," Cole said as calmly as if they were discussing what to have for dinner. He turned the key in the ignition and started the truck's engine. But instead of reaching for the gearshift to put it in reverse, he slid his hand around the back of her neck, tugging her toward him. His mouth came down on hers. He took his time, kissing her so thoroughly that Addie felt her toes actually curl inside her pumps.

"To think about on the way," he said when he released her.

As if she could do anything else, Addie thought, as he put the truck into gear and pulled out of the parking lot.

Chapter 9

Cole had acted on impulse when he asked Addie to come home with him. He'd spent a lot of time this past week thinking about her, about the taste of her, about how she'd felt in his arms. It had been a long time since a woman had absorbed so much of his thoughts.

He'd done some dating since his divorce, had even, once or twice, thought that it might go beyond dating, that the quick jolt of chemistry might turn into something more lasting. But when it hadn't, he'd felt scant regret. Between running Walker Air and raising his daughter, he'd had more than enough to occupy his time. And then Addie Smith literally crash-landed into his life and he was suddenly thinking about her more often than he liked to admit.

Sitting next to her at dinner, he'd been acutely aware of the delicate, floral scent of her perfume, of the soft cadences of her voice, of the warmth of her shoulder only inches from his. He'd enjoyed watching her reaction to his family. The Walkers en masse could be a little intimidating to the uninitiated but Addie had appeared more fascinated than overwhelmed.

He hadn't planned on asking her to come home with him until the two of them had been sitting in the truck and it had struck him that he didn't want to say goodnight. He wanted to hold her, wanted to kiss her, and he didn't know when the opportunity would come again.

It had made sense at the time, Cole thought, as he unlocked the front door of his house and ushered Addie inside. But he hadn't expected to feel as nervous as a kid contemplating his first time. Maybe he'd been out of the dating loop too long, he thought ruefully. He didn't know whether to offer her a glass of wine or suggest they check out the late-night television schedule or just do what he was aching to do, which was pull her into his arms and kiss her socks off.

"I thought bachelors were supposed to be bad housekeepers," Addie said, looking around the tidy living room.

"I am. But when Mary was about two, she was nearly swallowed whole by a pile of unfolded laundry and I figured I'd better mend my ways. The trick is to never let anything get too far out of hand. If I ever get tired of flying, I could probably write a book of household tips. How to get grape juice out of curtains and catsup stains out of your eyebrows—that kind of thing."

"Sounds like a great idea. Very politically correct to have a man writing something like that."

"I'll keep it in mind." He reached out and caught her hand in his, tugging her closer. "You don't really want to talk about my housekeeping skills, do you?"

"N-no." Addie's response was breathless, her eyes wide and a little uneasy.

Cole's unexpected attack of nervousness disappeared as quickly as it had appeared. She was looking at him as if half expecting him to pounce on her and ravish her on the spot. While he wouldn't deny that the idea held a certain appeal, he could see that Addie didn't feel the same.

"You only have to say the word and I'll take you home," he told her, praying that she wouldn't take him up on his offer.

Addie felt a shiver of awareness run down her spine as she looked up at him. All during the nearly silent drive here, she'd told herself that she knew what she was doing. It wasn't as if she were a trembling virgin, unaware of even the basics of what was about to happen. Come to think of it, in this day and age, even virgins were bound to know the mechanics and they probably didn't tremble much, either.

But when she'd walked into Cole's house and heard him shut the door behind her, she'd felt a quick flash of purely feminine fear. It wasn't that she was afraid of Cole exactly. She knew he wouldn't hurt her. But she was suddenly aware that her experiences with Duane might not have really prepared her for going to bed with a man of Cole's experience. What if she did something wrong? What if she was clumsy and he found her gauche and boring? If she hadn't been able to hold Duane's attention, how could she possibly expect to hold Cole's?

"I've done this before," she said abruptly. "I'm twenty-seven. No woman is a virgin at twenty-seven these days."

She saw Cole's eyes widen in surprise and then his mouth curved in a slow smile.

"Is there a law against it?" His thumb stroked over the pulse beating so erratically in her wrist while his other hand lifted to her hair, his fingers finding the pins that held a slightly crooked French twist in place at the back of her head.

"N-no." Addie's response was shaky as he began pulling the pins loose, letting them fall to the floor. "I just didn't want you to think that I'm not experienced."

"I'm glad you warned me," he said solemnly. He threaded his fingers through her hair, loosening it until the silky brown strands fell down around her shoulders.

She'd never thought of the scalp as an erogenous zone but she could feel his touch all the way to her toes. Her breath caught as he bent his head and began planting feather-soft kisses down the side of her face, his mouth brushing hers lightly once, twice and then lingering, coaxing her lips to open for him so that his tongue could slip inside, tasting the sweet warmth of her response.

When he lifted his head, Addie's fingers were clinging to his shoulders, her body curved into his in wordless surrender. She opened her eyes slowly and stared up into his face. "I'm not very good at this," she said breathlessly.

"Oh?" Cole's dark brows arched in question. "How do you figure?"

"Duane."

"Duane?" He began unbuttoning the pearl buttons that marched down the front of her dusty blue silk blouse. "There's really a person named Duane?"

"He's the one . . . He and I . . ."

"The man with whom you acquired all your vast experience?" he suggested, taking pity on her inability to find the right words.

Her blouse was open to the waist but he wasn't sure she'd realized it yet. She was so intent on giving him a careful history of her past sexual experience. He supposed that a more sensitive man might be offended or possibly threatened by her bringing up an old boyfriend in the midst of his own seduction but he couldn't help but find her solemn determination to make a clean breast of everything more amusing than threatening.

"Not vast," Addie said, not wanting to give him the wrong impression. "There was just Duane and we . . . it was only . . . I'm just not very good at this," she finished half-defiantly.

"According to Duane?"

She nodded miserably.

"I tell you what, why don't we forget all about Duane." He traced the upper edge of her bra with the tip of one finger. She jerked in surprise at the feel of him touching her breast. "I have a strong suspicion that Duane might not have been the expert he led you to believe. What do you think?''

''M-maybe.'' Addie had to swallow to get the single word out. Certainly she'd never felt anything with Duane that came close to what she was feeling now. Cole's fingertip brushed across the soft swell of her breast, light as a feather, barely touching her skin and yet she could feel a shivery awareness working its way down her spine.

''Do you trust me?'' he asked. His breath stirred the fine tendrils of hair at her temple. His thumb brushed lightly across the peak of her breast, teasing her nipple through the thin fabric of her bra. Addie felt her whole body tremble in response.

''Yes.'' She gave him the answer without hesitation. She trusted him completely.

''Good.'' He leaned down, his mouth swallowing her soft gasp of surprise as his hands caught her knees and shoulders and he scooped her off her feet to carry her into his bedroom.

What followed bore no resemblance to her previous experiences. For the first time Addie realized what a disservice she'd done herself in allowing her first— and only—lover to so influence her opinion of her own sexuality. Cole took her image of herself as cold and sexually repressed and turned it inside out to reveal a woman capable of deep passion and powerful response.

With Duane, sex had been both awkward and mechanical. Addie had never quite known what to do with her arms, never known where to put her hands, had never been sure what was expected of her. She'd felt clumsy and inept, though, looking back with the advantage of years, she suspected that she'd felt no more inept than her partner.

There were none of those moments of clumsiness with Cole. From the moment he set her down beside his bed, he controlled their lovemaking with gentle strength. Her clothes seemed to disappear as if by magic. He gave her no chance to feel self-conscious about her nudity, no opportunity to remember her body's flaws, either real or imagined. His hands skimmed over her from shoulder to thigh.

"You are so beautiful," he said quietly.

And, in that moment, with him looking at her as if he'd never seen a more desirable woman, Addie felt beautiful and desirable.

"Aren't you overdressed?" she asked, her smile trembling a little around the edges.

Cole's fingers were not quite steady as he unbuttoned his shirt. There was something incredibly arousing in the thought that he wanted her so much that he trembled with it. With that knowledge came a feeling of empowerment like nothing she'd ever known before. She felt as if she were the very essence of feminine power.

She reached out to tug at the buckle of his belt. His breath caught, his stomach jerking inward as her fingers brushed against his skin, and Addie felt her own power rise like a soft, warm flood within her. Pulling open his belt, she reached for the tab of his zipper, but Cole's hand closed over hers, stopping her.

"If we don't slow down, this is going to be over before it begins," he warned her in a voice gone raspy with need. When she gave him a blank look, uncertain of his meaning, he shifted her hand downward so that her fingers cupped the heavy bulge of his erection. ''It's been a while for me and I want you so damned much, I'm about to explode.''

The blunt explanation made her flush but she didn't pull away. Instead her hand moved, tracing the thick length of him through the fabric of his jeans. Watching her, Cole thought he'd never seen anything more erotic than the dawning awareness of her own sexual potential. He caught her hand, pressing it against his aching flesh with convulsive strength before pushing her away.

''You're going to be the death of me,'' he muttered, gathering the tattered threads of his self-control. Her fingers found his zipper again and began easing it downward. He gritted his teeth and surrendered to the inevitable. ''On the other hand, it's a hell of a way to go. Just let me get my damned boots off.''

He scooped her up and set her down on the bed. Addie watched as he sat on the edge of the bed. His boots hit the floor with twin thuds, followed in rapid succession by his socks and shirt. He stood and set his hands on his hips, shoving both jeans and briefs down with one smooth motion. When he straightened, Addie felt a quick surge of purely feminine uneasiness.

She knew the differences between the male and female body, of course. But the few hurried couplings with Duane had always occurred with the lights out and seeing a naked man in a magazine was a far cry from seeing one naked and heavily aroused, standing less than two feet away. She was caught off guard by a sudden awareness of the basic differences between man and woman. Male and female.

Cole slid into the bed next to her and she realized that their differences were all a part of the wonder. The hard planes and angles of his body complemented the softer curves of hers. The rasp of his beard against the delicate skin of her breast was an erotic contrast to the heat of his mouth closing over the puckered bud of her nipple. And then his lean body rose above hers, his muscular thighs parting her legs, and she felt the smooth heat of him press against the slick moisture of her most feminine flesh.

Addie caught her breath, her eyes widening in wonder as he sheathed himself within her in one slow, smooth stroke. She'd thought she knew what to expect, thought that, despite all the wonders he'd already shown her, this was the one thing that would hold no surprises. She couldn't have been more wrong.

Her body stretched to accommodate the heavy length of him, welcoming his possession as if made for him alone. She hadn't, until this moment, realized how empty she'd been, how hungry. But only for this man. Only for him.

It was like coming home, Cole thought, groaning at the feel of her soft inner muscles clasping him, welcoming him. It had never felt like this, never felt so completely right. He wanted to make it last forever, wanted to savor the soft friction of their bodies straining together. But Addie's body was arching to meet his, her small hands clinging to his shoulders. She was trembling on the edge of fulfillment, her body straining toward it. He could have chosen to prolong

the moment, to draw out her pleasure as well as his
own. But he wanted—needed—to feel her come apart
in his arms, needed to see the wonder in her eyes when
she finally discovered what it was she was reaching for.

Addie gasped as Cole slid his hands beneath her
bottom, pulling her upward so that she took him more
deeply within her. Tension coiled within her, tight and
hard. There was something...something so close. She
strained to reach it, to touch it. And then it was suddenly there—sensations cascading one into the next,
drenching her body in a pleasure so intense that it
hovered on the fine edge of pain.

She cried out, arching against Cole, her inner muscles tightening around him in delicate but irresistible
demand, tumbling him headlong into the whirlpool of
her pleasure. With a groan, he surrendered to the
aching need, shuddering in her arms as his body
pulsed within hers. Together, they tumbled into the
spinning magic, linked body and soul as they shared
their fulfillment.

It was a very long time before Cole gathered the energy to move. A pleasant lethargy sapped the strength
from his arms and legs. He felt replete, comfortably
lazy and he would have been content to lie just where
he was for the next thirty or forty years. But sooner or
later, Addie was bound to want to breathe again. She
moaned a soft protest as he eased himself away. Her
hands clung to his back, urging him back down.

"Let me go, honey. I'll crush you."

"I don't care," she mumbled.

"Well, I do," Cole said with a smile in his voice.

He collapsed onto the bed and slid one arm under her, pulling her close. Addie snuggled against him, resting her head on his shoulder, one hand resting on his chest. They lay without speaking for a little while. It was Cole who eventually broke the comfortable silence.

"You know what?"

"What?" Addie wondered idly if it was possible to expire from contentment.

"Duane was wrong."

It was so unexpected that her eyes flew open and she tilted her head back to look up at him.

"What?"

"The guy who made you think you weren't good at this." Cole's eyes twinkled with warm laughter. "He was soo-oo wrong."

Addie felt a flush start somewhere around her toes and work its way upward until her whole body turned warm with the heat of it.

"I can't believe I told you about Duane," she muttered.

"I thought it was very kind of you to warn me," he said, mock solemn. He wasn't making fun of her. Instead, he was inviting her to share the joke. Looking back on her babbled confessions, Addie was torn between laughter and embarrassment. She felt light-years removed from that woman.

"I should have kept my mouth shut."

"I appreciated your honesty," Cole said. "Not everyone would have had the integrity to— Ouch!"

"Not another word about Duane," she warned, releasing the chest hairs she'd just tugged.

"You don't have to get violent about it. Actually, there was just one more thing I wanted to say." He took the precaution of catching her hand in his. "Poor old Duane missed out on a hell of a lot."

Addie looked at him and felt her mouth curve in slow smile. "He did, didn't he?"

And that was another thing Duane had been wrong about—laughter and sex *did* go together.

Chapter 10

"I'm so glad you could come over," Kelsey said as she led the way into the kitchen. "I felt terrible about interrupting the celebration dinner like that. When Nikki said she was driving up from L.A. to see the baby, it seemed like the perfect opportunity to make it up to you, at least partially."

"You don't have to make anything up to me," Addie protested. "I had a very nice time."

"Oh, I'm sure spending three hours at the hospital waiting for me to give birth is your idea of a perfect way to end an evening," Kelsey said, throwing a warm, mischievous smile over her shoulder.

Addie returned the smile and hoped that Kelsey wouldn't notice her suddenly heightened color. Her hostess had no way of knowing that her evening hadn't ended at the hospital. Nearly two weeks later, the memory of just how it *had* ended was enough to make her feel a little shivery inside.

"Well, at the very least, you should take a look at the cause of all the trouble," Kelsey said as they entered the kitchen.

"Are you implying that Lily could ever cause any trouble?" Nikki asked. She was seated at the table, the baby cradled in her arms. She looked up and gave Addie a welcoming smile before frowning at Kelsey. "Anyone can see that this child is a perfect angel. She's too sweet to cause trouble."

"You haven't heard the angel when she wants to be fed or wants her diaper changed," Kelsey said with a laugh. She bent to lift her daughter from Nikki's arms. "Say hello to Aunt Addie, pumpkin."

Addie threw her a startled look. *Aunt?* She'd never expected to be anyone's aunt, honorary or otherwise. But certainly she couldn't imagine having a sweeter niece, she thought, looking down at the infant. At not quite two weeks old, Lily Marie Walker was as exquisite as a porcelain doll. The pure ivory of her skin was a vivid contrast to the silky mat of almost black hair that covered her head. Her eyes were an indeterminate gray-blue but Addie was willing to bet that they were going to change to the same vivid electric blue as her father's. She blinked up at Addie, her tiny rosebud mouth puckered as if in thought.

"She's perfect," Addie whispered, awestruck.

"We like her," Kelsey said lightly. "Would you like to hold her?"

"May I?"

"Sure. She's not as breakable as she looks," Kelsey assured her as she transferred Lily into Addie's arms.

For several minutes the three women were completely occupied with admiring the baby. Lily accepted the attention as her due. She was already quite well aware that the world centered around her. When she yawned for the second time, Kelsey announced that it was time for a nap. Lifting the child from Addie's hold, she transferred her to the cradle that sat in one corner of the kitchen.

"How is Gage holding up?" Nikki asked as Kelsey tucked a light blanket around the drowsy baby.

"Not too bad. He still counts her fingers and toes at least once a day, but I've almost managed to convince him that she won't break at a touch. He's become her devoted slave, of course."

"Of course." Nikki laughed and shook her head. "There's nothing like a baby for bringing strong men to their knees. I'm looking forward to seeing Sam humbled on the altar of paternal slavery."

"Are you pregnant?" Kelsey exclaimed.

"Not yet but we're trying." Nikki's smile was oddly uncertain. "Nothing's happened yet but we've only been trying for a few months."

"Well, at least the trying is fun," Kelsey murmured wickedly. The three of them giggled like naughty children.

"I'm not complaining but I can't wait to see Sam as a nervous new father."

"It's something to see a grown man blanch at the thought of dealing with an eight-pound baby," Kelsey agreed. "I think Gage is a little more paranoid than most because of his sister."

"His sister?" Addie looked at her questioningly. "Cole has a sister?"

Kelsey exchanged glances with Nikki before answering. "A half sister, really. Shannon. She'd be... What? About twenty-four now?" She looked to Nikki for confirmation.

"Something like that."

"Is she...dead?" Addie asked hesitantly.

"No." It was Nikki who answered. "At least, not that anyone knows of. I don't think they even let themselves think about the possibility actually. You know that Rachel remarried after the boys' father died?"

Addie nodded. "Cole said that his stepfather was a bastard."

"That's putting it mildly," Nikki said, her expression grim. "From what Sam's told me, he beat the two younger boys and made life hell for all of them. Rachel realized what a mistake she'd made fairly quickly and got a divorce. Then she found out she was pregnant. They all adored the baby and probably spoiled her rotten. Her father had visitation rights, which he took sporadic advantage of. When Shannon was about four, he tried to talk Rachel into taking him back but she wouldn't have anything to do with him. Next thing they knew, he took Shannon for the weekend and just disappeared with her."

"Oh, how awful," Addie cried softly. "They didn't know where he'd taken her?"

"Didn't and still don't," Kelsey said. "Gage was looking after her the day his stepfather took Shannon and he blamed himself for letting her go."

"But he couldn't have been very old himself, surely," Addie protested.

"He was fifteen."

"Then how could he possibly think he was to blame?"

"It's a male thing," Kelsey said, as if that explained everything.

"How awful for all of them," Addie murmured. "Never to know what happened to her."

"Sam says he still puts inquiries out now and again," Nikki said. "Not that there's much hope of hearing anything after all these years."

"You never know," Kelsey said. "Shannon would be a grown woman by now. Maybe she's curious about her past. If she were to start making inquiries, she might run across something."

"It's nice to think so," Nikki said, but her tone made it clear that she thought the odds were against such a happy ending.

"Anything's possible," Kelsey said. Giving in to the compulsion to check on her own child, she got up from the table and went to peek into Lily's cradle. The infant was still sound asleep. "I can't imagine what it must be like to lose a child," she murmured, touching one flushed cheek with the tip of her finger.

The kitchen was silent for a moment as each of them contemplated the fragility of life. It was Nikki who broke the silence before it could grow oppressive.

"Enough of this depressing stuff," she said briskly. She pinned Addie with an inquisitive look, her green eyes sparkling with mischief. "What I want to know is how things are going with you and Cole."

"What things?" Addie could feel her cheeks flush even as she struggled to look unconcerned. "I don't know what you mean."

"She always was a terrible liar," Nikki told her sister-in-law. "She could never get involved in any plots to overthrow the school board or tar and feather the principal because as soon as anyone asked what was going on her eyes got that panic-stricken expression and she turned bright red."

"There's nothing wrong with having a naturally honest disposition," Addie said with careful dignity.

"Not as long as you stick to the truth," Nikki agreed. "But don't try to tell me that there isn't something going on between you and Cole. I saw the way you two looked at each other at dinner the other night."

"I... We have been seeing each other," Addie admitted.

"We guessed that much," Kelsey said as she got the pitcher of iced tea from the refrigerator and refilled their glasses. "What we want to know is—"

"Everything!" Nikki finished for her.

"There's not much to tell," Addie protested with a half laugh. "We've seen each other a few times. That's all."

"All?" Nikki's elegantly arched eyebrows rose. "The air was practically sizzling between the two of you at dinner."

"You're exaggerating," Addie mumbled. Her cheeks felt as if they were on fire.

"I am not. Am I exaggerating?" Nikki demanded of Kelsey.

"Definite sizzle," Kelsey said solemnly.

"Don't try to deny it," Nikki said sternly. "Tell us everything."

Addie's teeth worried at her lower lip as she debated with herself. She was too quiet and self-effacing to make friends easily. She and Nikki had been close in school, but in the years since graduation, they'd kept in touch with each other only sporadically. Still, she knew that, for all her teasing, Nikki would stand by her friend. She barely knew Kelsey Walker, but something told her that they could become friends. And she very much wanted to be able to confide at least some of what she was feeling in someone she could trust.

"We're seeing each other quite a bit," she admitted cautiously.

"How much is quite a bit?" Nikki demanded.

"Half a dozen times since that night at dinner," she said on a rush of breath.

"Half a dozen times in less than two weeks?" Nikki's brows rose again. "That's some pretty serious 'seeing.'"

"Do you think so?" Addie frowned, her teeth worrying her lip again. "I haven't...dated much and I thought... But then, I wasn't sure. Mary's always with us. I don't mind. She's so sweet and I think she likes me. I like her, anyway. But she's there and... I thought maybe Cole didn't want... But I know it's hard to find baby-sitters. And they're so close. Which is good. That they're close, I mean. But I wasn't sure... I thought he might not..." Her voice trailed off and she gave her companions a helpless look as words failed her.

"Let me see if I interpreted this correctly," Kelsey said, frowning in concentration. "You and Cole are seeing a lot of each other but, because he brings Mary along, you think he might be just looking for a companion for her?"

"Well, not exactly." Said out loud, it sounded rather foolish. "It's just that Mary likes me and we get along pretty well and—"

"And you're afraid he might have some ulterior motive for bringing her along?"

"Not *ulterior* exactly." Addie lifted her shoulders in a shrug. It all made sense in her head but it didn't seem to make much sense when she tried to explain it.

"Look, the fact that Cole is bringing her along is very significant," Nikki said. "He thinks the sun rises and sets on that little girl. He wouldn't let her get close to you, wouldn't even let her get to know you if he wasn't serious about you."

"Serious?" Addie's eyes widened in terror. She hadn't even dared *think* the word, let alone say it out loud. "I'm sure he's not... He couldn't be... It's just that he— We— The crash..." she got out finally, "We kind of got to know each other, that's all."

"Right," Nikki said, nodding as if she understood completely. "You got to know each other after the crash so, even though he's not attracted to you in any way whatsoever, he asks you out half a dozen times in less than two weeks and lets his daughter get close to you. Not to mention looks at you like a starving man eyeing a cream puff. Sure. Makes perfect sense to me.''

''Did he really look at me as if I were a cream puff?'' Addie asked, a pleased little smile curving her mouth.

''A deluxe model with chocolate frosting,'' Kelsey confirmed.

Their eyes met and all three burst into laughter.

''How come I have to stay with Mrs. Karlson?'' Mary asked for the fifth time in the past half hour.

''Because I'm taking Addie out for a grown-up meal. No plastic forks, no paper napkins and no McAnything,'' Cole explained patiently.

''Addie likes eating at McDonald's. She said so.''

''That doesn't mean she wants to eat there for the rest of her life.''

''I still don't see why I can't go with you.'' Mary's lower lip thrust out in the merest suggestion of a pout.

Cole had been attempting to comb some semblance of order into his hair but now he turned to look at his daughter. ''You can't come because I'm taking Addie out on a date. Little girls do not go with their fathers on dates.''

''We've done lots of stuff with her the last couple of weeks. Aren't those dates?''

''No. They're . . . get-togethers,'' he improvised hastily. ''A date is just for two people.''

The truth was, he hadn't had a chance to see Addie alone for more than a few minutes at a time since the night they'd made love and it was driving him nuts.

Being with her, seeing her, but not being able to touch her in any but the most casual of ways was pure torture.

"You needn't act as if you're being abandoned," he told his daughter. "Jenny Karlson is one of your best friends. I thought you'd enjoy spending the night at her house."

"I guess." Mary traced one finger along one of the black stripes woven into his bedspread.

Her long-suffering expression had Cole swallowing a grin as he turned back to the mirror. He should have made time to get a haircut, he thought as he dragged a comb through his hair.

"Maybe you could pick me up at Jenny's when you get back from your date?" Mary suggested. "Maybe you and Addie and me could play games or something?"

"It's going to be too late for that," he said firmly. He had other plans for the night, plans that did not include his seven-year-old daughter. He sincerely hoped to be bringing Addie back here and he had no intention of picking up Mary so they could all play a brisk round of Parcheesi. Giving up the idea of taming his hair, he pulled open the closet door and reached for a shirt. Pulling out a seldom worn dress shirt, he shook the hanger, hoping to shake a few of the wrinkles out.

He gave his daughter a speculative look. He'd been wanting to talk to her about Addie. He hadn't planned on doing it now, but if he'd learned one thing as a parent, it was that it wasn't smart to let opportunities pass you by.

"You like Addie, don't you?" He kept his tone casual, faintly disinterested.

"Yes." Mary was running her finger along a royal blue line now. "Her eyes always smile," she commented without looking up.

Cole felt a subtle easing of tension. He wasn't sure where his relationship with Addie was going but he wanted to get some idea of how Mary felt about it. It didn't sound as if she would object if things went further, if Addie became a bigger part of her life.

"She likes you, too." Cole said, maintaining his casual tone.

He was just congratulating himself on having sounded his daughter out without her being any the wiser, when Mary looked up at him, her dark eyes shrewd.

"Are you guys going to get married?"

"Married?" Cole felt as if she'd just kicked him in the solar plexus. *Married?* Who had said anything about marriage? He'd just wanted to sound out her feelings about Addie in case he...in case they... Damn, if he hadn't been thinking about marriage, what *had* been on his mind?

"I— Nobody said anything about marriage," he muttered. Turning, he dove back into the closet, speaking over his shoulder. "For one thing, Addie and I haven't really known each other all that long."

"Grandma says it doesn't always take a long time to know you love someone," Mary said, sounding much older than her years.

"She did, did she?" *Thanks, Mom.* Cole groped for a tie. Since he rarely wore one, they were stuffed on a hanger that had been shoved to the back of his closet.

"Grandma says that sometimes all you have to do is look at someone to know you love them," Mary continued, clearly enjoying her role as a dispenser of romantic wisdom.

"I think Grandma has been watching too many soap operas," Cole said, finally getting his hands on the hangerful of ties and pulling it forth in triumph. "Love doesn't always work that way, pumpkin."

"You said you loved me as soon as you saw me," Mary said, demonstrating the uncanny ability of children to remember things slightly out of context and apply them to a given discussion in such a way as to put their parents in the position of either agreeing that they'd said something they hadn't *really* said or disagreeing and admitting that they'd lied, when they hadn't done that, either.

"That was different," Cole said, falling back on the only safe response. He scowled at the rack of ties. Maybe it was time he updated his wardrobe a bit. He didn't seem to have much by way of suitable attire for dating in the nineties.

"How was it different?" Mary asked with a tenacity at odds with her delicate appearance.

Cole threw the ties, hanger and all, on the bed next to the wrinkled shirt and gave his full attention to his daughter. "It's different because you were my little girl and I loved you the minute I saw you."

"Was I all red and wrinkly like Aunt Kelsey's baby?" She looked doubtful.

"You were red and wrinkly and you started screaming like a banshee as soon as they put you in my arms and I thought you were beautiful."

"Yech." Mary wrinkled her nose and Cole grinned.

"Now that I think about it, you were pretty gross," he said.

She giggled. "Maybe you should have traded me in on a cuter kid."

"Nah." He sat down on the bed and slid his arm around her, pulling her close. "I knew I had the best one."

She leaned into his hold and he was suddenly, almost painfully aware of how fast she was growing up. It seemed like less than a heartbeat ago that she'd been just big enough to fit in his two hands. It wouldn't be much more than that before she was ready to start dating. The thought scared the hell out of him.

"So, does that mean you don't love Addie?" she asked, circling back to the original topic with the determination of a bulldog.

Good question, Cole acknowledged. He would have given a great deal to know the answer. He knew he cared for her, knew he wanted to spend time with her. He missed her when she wasn't around, felt better when she was. He wanted to see her smile, wanted to take care of her whether she needed him to or not. And if that wasn't love, what the hell was it?

"I don't know," he said. He wasn't sure it was an honest answer but it was the only one he was prepared to give. He looked down at her. "Would you mind if I did?"

Mary hesitated a moment. She looked down, her slim fingers picking at an imaginary spot on the knee of her jeans. "I guess not," she said, making it clear that her father wasn't the only one who was less than certain about his feelings. "Addie's real nice."

"Yes, she is."

"And I wouldn't mind having a mom. Not that I *mind* not having one," she added quickly. She looked up at him, her brown eyes earnest. "You and I are a family all by ourselves."

Cole felt his heart crack a little at her obvious concern that she might have hurt his feelings. His arm tightened around her. "We are a family," he agreed. "But there's nothing wrong with wanting a mom, honey. You know I love your grandma, but that doesn't mean I didn't wish that I had a dad, too."

Mary nodded to indicate that she understood what he was telling her. They sat in silence for a moment, her head resting on his shoulder, his arm around her. Cole glanced at the clock and tightened his arm around her for a second before releasing her.

"If I don't get moving, I'm going to be late." Dropping a kiss on the top of her head, he rose from the bed.

"Daddy?"

"What?" His tone was absent. How was it possible to have a drawer full of socks and not have any two that matched? He poked cautiously among the tangle of browns and blacks and grays, looking for two socks that looked as if they might actually belong together.

"My mom—Roxie—did she go away because of me?"

Cole's fingers clenched around the edge of the drawer and for a moment his mind went completely blank. Mary rarely mentioned her mother. As far as he knew, she didn't think about Roxie any more often, which suited him just fine. Forcing his fingers to release their death grip on the pale oak and schooling his expression to one of mild interest, he turned to look at her.

"Your mom went away because she and I decided that we couldn't be together anymore. It had nothing to do with you."

It was half the truth. There was no way he could explain to a seven-year-old that her mother simply hadn't wanted her. Roxie had agreed to go through with the pregnancy because he'd wanted the baby, but she'd wanted nothing to do with motherhood. They'd divorced shortly after Mary was born, with no real regret on either side.

"Tammy Sinclair's mom and dad got a divorce when she was a baby," Mary said. She didn't look at him but focused her attention on the pattern in the bedspread, tracing it with one small finger. "She lives with her mom but she still sees her dad pretty often. She says it's weird that I never see my mom."

"Not everyone is good at being a parent," Cole said, choosing his words carefully. "Your mom was just one of those people who isn't really meant to have kids. She knew that and she knew how much I wanted you and that I'd take good care of you. So she left you with me because we both thought it was best for you."

Which was also a half-truth. Roxie hadn't been nearly as concerned with what was best for her baby as she had been with what was best for herself, but it had all worked out the same in the end. He wished he could see his daughter's expression but she was looking down at the careful movement of her hand and all he could see was the top of her head.

"We've talked about this before, Mary. What made you bring it up now?"

"Nothin'," She hunched her shoulders.

"Nothin'?" Cole's tone was doubtful. "Must have been something. Was it just what Tammy said?"

Another shrug. She continued to trace the lines in the bedspread. Watching her, Cole promised himself that he'd never again buy a bedspread that had any pattern in it—solid colors only from here on out. He pushed himself away from the dresser and moved back over to the bed. Mary didn't look up when he sat down.

"Did your friend Tammy say anything else?" he asked, taking a shot in the dark.

"She's not my friend," Mary muttered.

"Okay. Did Tammy who's not your friend say anything else?"

She shrugged again. "Nothing important."

"What did she say?" Cole knew they were finally approaching the heart of the problem.

"Stupid stuff."

"What kind of stupid stuff?" he asked. One thing he'd learned in the last seven years was that patience and persistence were essential to prying information out of children.

"It was dumb." Mary's tone was elaborately unconcerned but Cole wasn't fooled.

"I don't mind hearing dumb stuff."

She shot him a quick glance from under her lashes and then returned her attention to the pattern on the spread. "She said that my mom doesn't want to see me because of my heart. She said that it was because I was practically a cripple and that my mom didn't want nothing to do with me."

For a brief moment, Cole allowed himself to contemplate the joys of laying the flat of his hand against the unknown Tammy's rear end, but revenge, even if possible, was not as important as repairing the damage wrought by her childishly cruel remarks.

"First of all, you're not a cripple, practically or otherwise." He kept his tone calm and chose his words with care. "And even if you were handicapped, that wouldn't have anything to do with why your mom isn't around. She didn't even know about the problem with your heart when she left."

"She didn't?" Mary lifted her head to look at him and the vulnerability in her eyes made his heart ache.

"She didn't." Mary's heart condition *hadn't* had anything to do with Roxie's decision to leave. And finding out about it hadn't changed her mind. So if it was technically a lie, it wasn't one in spirit. "So Tammy Whatsit doesn't know what she's talking about," he finished firmly.

"Tammy's dumb," she muttered. "Nobody listens to her."

"Well, if she always says things that are silly, nobody should."

She nodded and continued to trace the patterns on the spread. Cole waited. He knew her well enough to know there was something else on her mind.

"If you and Addie got married—"

"We haven't even talked about that," Cole reminded her, but the thought sounded a little less startling the second time around.

"I know. But if you *did,* do you think you guys'd have more kids?"

God, first she was marrying him off, now she was adding to the family! Cole was torn between laughter and panic. He didn't even know what he wanted and she was already arranging his future.

"Since I don't even know if we're going to get married, don't you think it's a little early to start thinking about kids?"

"If you did, though," she said insistently. "You might have kids."

"We might," he agreed cautiously, wondering where this was going. "Why are you so concerned about these imaginary children?"

"I just thought that if you had other kids... Well, they'd probably have good hearts and then... Well, you might wish..."

"Hold it right there!" Cole scooped her up off the bed and set her down on his lap, wrapping his arms around her and holding her close. "I wouldn't wish anything at all because I couldn't possibly wish for anything else when I've got you."

"But if they had good hearts—"

"You've got the best heart of anybody I've ever known," he said firmly. He blinked against the burning sensation in his eyes and set his hand under her chin, tilting her face up to his. "I couldn't love you any more if you had two absolutely perfect hearts."

She giggled. "I couldn't have *two* hearts, Daddy. There isn't room."

"It wouldn't matter if there were because I couldn't possibly love you more than I already do. And *if* Addie and I got married and *if* we had another child, that wouldn't change the way I feel about you at all. I'm always going to love you best of all. Okay?"

"Okay." She relaxed against him, pressing her cheek to his chest, her fingers twisting one of the buttons on his shirt.

"Daddy?"

"Yes?"

"I think it would be nice if you married Addie."

Cole smiled over her head. "I'm starting to think so, too."

"Daddy?"

"Yeah?"

"I think you're sitting on your shirt."

Chapter 11

Addie walked downstairs slowly. The heels on her new shoes were higher than she usually wore and she didn't want to begin the evening by tripping over her own feet and tumbling to the bottom of the stairs. Especially not now when the shivery feeling in the pit of her stomach was telling her that this was going to be a special night.

Reaching the foyer, she glanced at the mahogany grandfather clock that stood against one wall. Looming over the entry, all dark wood and heavy scrollwork, it had always seemed to her to be wearing a permanent expression of disapproval. When she was a child, she'd been a little afraid of it and had made it a point to give it a wide berth. Tonight, she stuck her tongue out at its overdecorated face before continuing on her way into the living room.

She was looking forward to her date with Cole tonight, their first since the night Kelsey's baby was born, the night they'd become lovers. Every time she'd seen him since then, Mary had been included. She'd enjoyed the chance to get to know his daughter, finding the little girl, in her own way, every bit as charming as her father. But one could hardly advance the course of an affair with a seven-year-old child looking on.

An affair. Addie's mouth curved in a small, secretive smile. Astonishing as it seemed, she was actually having an affair with Cole Walker. Even more amazing, she was starting to think there was a chance that it could become something much more than just an affair. Her talk with Kelsey and Nikki this afternoon had made her realize that they were right—Cole wouldn't pull Mary into his relationship with her unless it was one that he valued.

Addie ran her fingers along the piecrust edge of a whatnot table, her eyes dreamy. A month ago she'd thought romance was out of her life, more or less permanently. In twenty-seven years, Duane was as close to a romantic entanglement as she'd come and there had been no reason to think anything more exciting loomed on the horizon.

But the plane crash had changed everything. It had made Cole Walker a part of her life. Whatever did— or didn't—happen now, she was changed—by the crash and all that had happened since.

"Are you going out tonight?"

At the sound of her father's voice, Addie started and turned. Looking at him, standing in the door-

way, tall and lean, his gray hair gleaming in the lamp-
light, she remembered how, when she was a little girl,
she'd thought she had the most handsome father in the
world. She couldn't help but feel a little bit that way
now.

"Cole is picking me up in a few minutes," she told
him. Though he'd never made any secret of his complete indifference to fashion, she couldn't resist the
urge to show off her new dress. She moved into the
center of the room and held the rich fabric of her skirt
out from her body. "What do you think?"

He looked at her, his expression shuttered. Addie
knew she was looking her best. She'd always compared herself to mother's delicate beauty and found
herself wanting. But tonight, the reflection in her
mirror had surprised her. She would never be the
beauty that Eileen Smith had been but the woman in
the mirror had been more than passable. In fact, she'd
been almost pretty.

The dress she'd purchased the day before suited her
more than anything else she'd ever owned. The cut was
simple and the garment was bare of ornamentation,
but the heavy silk fabric was a rich, clear blue that
made her skin look like pure ivory and brought out the
blue of her eyes. It had been outrageously expensive
and worth every penny. She'd applied her makeup
carefully and with a light hand—nothing more than a
brush of mascara to darken her lashes, a hint of coral
blush to highlight the curve of her cheekbone and a
smooth layer of soft red lipstick. The effect was nature taken one step better.

Looking at her now, Ronald Smith saw the same thing his daughter had seen in the mirror—a pretty young woman, wearing a lovely dress, her soft brown hair caught up in a simple twist at the back of her neck. But he saw something she hadn't—he saw a warmth in her eyes that hadn't been there before. The soft, slightly dreamy look of a woman in love, the tentative hopefulness of a woman who thought that love might be returned. He frowned.

"You've been seeing a great deal of this man, haven't you?"

"Yes." Addie hardly noticed that he hadn't commented on her appearance. She hadn't really expected him to do so. "It's mostly been the three of us getting together."

"The three of you?" he asked.

"He has a little girl, remember? Mary? I told you about her."

"Hmm." He didn't seem interested in hearing anything more about Mary. "Are you and this man, Walker, serious?"

Addie flushed. She felt an almost superstitious dread at hearing her hopes spoken out loud. "I... don't really know," she said. Her teeth tugged at her lower lip a moment and when she smiled, it was with a mixture of hope and fear. "I'd like to think so."

"I see." He slid his hands into the pockets of his slacks, his dark brows nearly meeting over the bridge of his aquiline nose. "Don't you think things are moving rather quickly? You haven't actually known each other very long."

"Not in terms of days or weeks maybe," she admitted. "But the time we spent in the mountains sort of accelerated things."

"You don't think it might perhaps have distorted your judgment, given you a mistaken feeling of... affinity for this man?"

"No, I don't," she said. The quick bluntness of her answer drew a thin line between her father's brows. She half expected him to pursue the argument, perhaps point out to her how foolish it would be to rush into something that could affect the rest of her life. But he surprised her.

"Well, I'm sure you're the best judge of that," he said. "Actually, I was hoping we'd get a chance to speak tonight. I have something I'd like to talk to you about and you've been gone so much lately that there hasn't been much opportunity."

He smiled thinly to show that he was not reproaching her. Addie could have pointed out that she'd spent almost every morning working with him in his den, but she didn't. She knew that, when he was working, he barely noticed the existence of anyone or anything outside the confines of what he was putting on paper.

"What did you want to talk to me about?" She stole a quick look at the mantel clock and hoped that Cole wasn't going to be late.

"I have decided to make a trip to the Soviet Union next month. There are some artifacts I'd like to examine and I'd like to take a closer look at some of the research that's been done by Soviet paleontologists. I think it could be very helpful."

"It sounds like a fascinating trip," Addie said, wondering what this had to do with her.

"I'd like you to come with me."

"What?" Addie stared at him in shock. He had never taken her with him when he traveled. After her mother's death, she'd begged him to let her accompany him on one of his numerous trips to gather research materials or examine one of the far-flung archaeological sites that might offer support for his theories about man's arrival on the North American continent. He'd always refused and by the time she graduated from college she'd quit asking. She'd traveled *for* him but never with him. Now he was suddenly offering her a lifelong dream.

"You want me to go with you?" she asked incredulously.

"I think you could be very valuable to me on this trip," he told her. "You're an excellent research assistant and you have quite a knack for getting through a great deal of material in a reasonably short amount of time."

"In English, maybe, but I don't speak Russian."

"The skills remain," he said, waving one elegant hand to dismiss the problems of language. "It wouldn't be all work, of course. I'm sure there would be plenty of time for sight-seeing."

"It sounds wonderful," Addie said. She felt a little dazed by this sudden offer. It was the first time he'd asked her to go anywhere with him and the first time he'd given any indication that he considered her skills as a research assistant anything better than average.

"Then you'll come." The words hovered somewhere between a statement and a question.

"Well, I—"

The doorbell rang before she could finish her sentence, which was probably just as well because she
didn't know what she was going to say. Moments before, Addie would have rushed to answer the door,
anxious to see Cole. Now, her head spinning with the
implications of her father's request, she stared blankly
in the direction of the foyer.

"I'll get it," Ronald said when she didn't move.

But by the time he led Cole into the living room,
Addie had recovered from her shock enough to greet
him.

"You look terrific," he said, the smile in his eyes
warming her.

"Thank you. You look very nice, too." This was the
first time she'd seen him in anything dressier than
slacks and a casual shirt. The charcoal gray suit, blue
shirt and conservatively striped tie made him seem
oddly unfamiliar.

"Are you going somewhere special?" Ronald
asked, lifting one brow in question.

"There's a new restaurant just opened that's supposed to be quite good," Cole answered. His tone was
polite but cool.

This was only the second time he and her father had
crossed paths and this meeting was showing no more
sign of warmth than the first, Addie thought. Though
he hadn't said as much, she suspected that Cole
thought her father had shown a callous of lack of
concern when he failed to meet her at the airport af-

ter their return. After meeting his family, she understood how he felt, but not everyone was like the Walkers. Her father was...different. But that certainly didn't mean he didn't love her.

"I'm really looking forward to dinner," she said, stepping between the two men both physically and verbally.

"Then I'll let you go." Ronald nodded pleasantly to Cole. "A pleasure," he murmured.

"Likewise," Cole said, stretching his lips in a smile that didn't reach his eyes. Addie was glad they were leaving.

It was drizzling halfheartedly, not heavy enough for rain, too heavy for mist, just a pervasive trickle of moisture that made life difficult without depositing enough rain to water plants or replenish the always thirsty aquifers. Huddled under Cole's umbrella, they hurried out to the curb where his truck was parked. He opened Addie's door for her and then hurried around to the driver's side. The door shut behind him, closing them in the warm dark interior.

"You look incredible," Cole said, turning in his seat to look at her.

"You already said that," Addie said, flushing with pleasure.

"No, I said you looked terrific," he corrected her. She caught the white gleam of his teeth against the darkness.

"My mistake," she apologized, feeling happiness bubble up inside her. One of the things she loved most about him was the fact that he laughed so often and so easily. She'd never known anyone who laughed as much as he did. And she'd never laughed as much with anyone else.

"I'll forgive you this time," he told her. "But it's going to cost you."

"How much?" But since he was already reaching for her, she had a pretty good idea of what the price would be. His hand closed around the back of her neck, pulling her half out of her seat as he leaned toward her. Addie's breath left her in a sigh of pleasure and relief as his mouth closed over hers.

There had been one or two stolen kisses in the last week but they hadn't been enough to satisfy. This kiss was long and slow and thorough and when he finally released her, Addie sank back down in her seat, feeling deliciously limp and boneless.

"I've been wanting to do that all week," Cole said huskily.

"Me, too." Addie's cheeks warmed at the shamelessness of her admission, but Cole didn't seem shocked.

"I don't think I'd ever realized just how in the way a seven-year-old could be."

"I didn't mind," Addie said quickly. "I like Mary."

"I'm pretty fond of her myself," he said, his teeth gleaming white in a quick smile. "But I was very glad to be able to get rid of her for a night."

"Me, too," Addie admitted with a quick, soft laugh.

Cole grinned again and then turned to put the key in the ignition. "This restaurant is supposed to be terrific," he said as pulled away from the curb.

"What kind of food do they serve?"

"Nouveau French, which probably means that they give you two tablespoons of substances of unrecognizable origin, exquisitely arranged on a pristine white plate."

"Probably." Addie didn't really care what they ate.

"They're starting to buy a few of their vegetables from Kelsey."

"It sounds like her business is doing well."

"From what Gage tells me, she could sell more if she could grow more. But she's got about all that she can handle, what with Danny and the new baby, plus the business."

"I had lunch with her and Nikki today."

"Did you?" Cole glanced at her, his expression interested. "I haven't been over in a week or so. How's she doing?"

"Good. The baby is adorable."

They talked a little about the baby, about Kelsey's business, about the work Cole was doing on the new plane, which he was trying to sandwich in around keeping his business going. The conversation segued from there to some of Mary's experiences in school. But all the time they were talking, Addie felt an almost painful awareness of Cole sitting just a little way away from her. She had only to stretch out her hand to touch him. The knowledge made her fingers tighten over the small black evening purse in her lap.

She found herself watching Cole's hands on the wheel and thinking about how those same hands had felt on her body, the skill with which his fingers had touched her, aroused her. Swallowing, she looked away, fixing her gaze firmly on the view out the rain-streaked windshield. She was a little shocked by this sudden discovery of her own, previously unsuspected, sexuality. For so long she'd thought of herself as sexually barren. Then Cole had shown her just how wrong she'd been. Now, just thinking about his touch was enough to make her skin tingle with awareness.

Wrapped in her own thoughts, Addie was only half-aware of the conversation fading away. It wasn't until Cole turned into the parking lot in front of the restaurant and pulled into a parking space that she realized neither of them had spoken in the past several minutes. He shut off the engine but made no move to open his door. Addie didn't move, either, not even to draw a breath. She was suddenly aware of an almost painful tension filling the truck, wrapping around the two of them—an almost tangible presence in the air.

Cole's fingers tightened on the steering wheel. He turned to look at her and Addie felt the air leave her lungs at the naked hunger in his expression.

"Are you hungry?" he asked. His voice held a guttural edge that tightened the knot building in Addie's stomach.

"Not particularly."

"Neither am I." He didn't move but simply sat there, his eyes all but devouring her. "I wanted to make this a special night."

"I don't need food for that," she whispered.

"Neither do I." Cole turned the key in the ignition almost violently.

It took twenty minutes to get from the restaurant to Cole's house. Neither of them said a word. By the time he pulled the car into his driveway there was a heavy, liquid heat in the pit of Addie's stomach. He hadn't touched her. Hadn't even spoken to her and she was almost painfully aroused. He opened his car door and she did the same. They met in front of the truck, their bodies colliding with delicious force.

"I was going to open your door," Cole said, his hands sliding down her back to flatten against her bottom.

"I didn't want to wait." Addie's fingers slid into his hair.

Cole's mouth came down on hers in a deep, soul-devouring kiss. His tongue plunged inside to tangle with hers in erotic imitation of the more intimate act they both craved. Addie's breasts were crushed against his chest and she could feel the iron-hard ridge of his arousal pressed against her belly through the layers of their clothing. She felt a deep, visceral ache inside and shifted, pressing closer, tearing a ragged groan from his throat. He dragged his mouth from hers and stared down at her.

"We're getting wet."

"I don't care." Her fingers tugged at the knot on his tie.

"If we don't get inside, we're going to give the neighbors a hell of a shock," he said. As he spoke, his hands were inching downward, his fingers finding the hem of her skirt and sliding beneath it. The feel of his hand on her thigh, with only the fragile barrier of her panty hose separating them, made Addie whimper softly.

"You're killing me," Cole groaned against her mouth.

Afterward, Cole couldn't remember exactly how he'd managed to get the two of them into the house. He did know that Addie was not much help. He remembered trying to get the key in the lock, fumbling when Addie's fingers found his belt and began loosening the buckle. He remembered cursing when the key wouldn't turn and her soft giggle when the door finally opened and they all but fell across the threshold.

His suit jacket hit the floor immediately, followed by his tie and Addie's shoes. The remainder of their clothing formed a trail leading to his bedroom. By the time they reached the bed, his entire body was aching with hunger. He stripped the last of their clothing away, only half-aware of her panty hose tearing as he pulled them from her, barely hearing the thud as his shoes hit the floor halfway across the room. And then he was tumbling her onto the bed, following her down, feeling her small body all soft and yielding beneath his.

Her hands came up to grasp his shoulders, her legs opening to him in an invitation as old as time. Without another second's delay, Cole sheathed himself in her. Addie's breath caught, her body arching in welcome and he knew he'd come home.

The hunger was too intense for it to last long. They moved together in an ancient rhythm, racing toward the beckoning fulfillment, finding it in one cataclysmic moment, tumbling headlong into the pleasure, clinging to each other as they rode the wave together before finally settling back down to earth.

For a long time, the only sound in the room was the ragged rasp of their breathing and the soft patter of the rain against the windows. Cole finally gathered the strength to lift his head from Addie's shoulder. He looked down at her.

"I guess I should cancel our reservations," he said.

She stared up at him a moment and then her mouth curved in a sweetly sensuous smile. Her fingers drifted across the damp skin of his back. "I guess you should," she agreed. "It doesn't look like we're going to make it out for dinner."

"I'll order a pizza later," Cole promised just before his mouth closed over hers.

They ate pizza at midnight, a slightly soggy creation delivered by a surly delivery boy who looked as if he'd rather be doing almost anything else. They devoured the mediocre pizza with as much enthusiasm as if it were a gourmet special. Addie couldn't remember when she'd last enjoyed a meal more but she knew that pleasure had little to do with the food and everything to do with the man sitting across the table from her.

"This is, quite possibly, the worst pizza I have ever eaten," Cole commented as he reached for a third slice.

"I'm glad to see that it hasn't killed your appetite."

"I'm just trying to keep up my strength." He grinned lasciviously and Addie laughed, even as she felt color flood her face.

Looking at her, Cole was struck by how pretty she looked. With her soft brown hair tumbled around her face, her blue eyes alight with laughter and her skin flushed from lovemaking, she looked so invitingly feminine that it was all he could do to resist the urge to sweep her up out of her chair and carry her back to bed.

It was hard to believe that, in less than a month, she'd become such an integral part of his life. His talk with Mary this afternoon had made him realize just how integral Addie had become in both their lives.

Don't you love Addie? He hadn't known how to answer his daughter but he knew how to answer the question for himself. He did love her. More than he'd thought possible. *Are you and Addie going to get married?* That question was a little more difficult. Marriage was a big step, a step he wasn't sure he was ready to take, for Mary's sake, as much as his own.

Their conversation earlier today had made him realize that her mother's desertion had left deeper scars than he'd realized. He couldn't risk her being hurt again. He had to take things slowly. Maybe he'd moved too fast as it was, bringing Addie into her life. She was already fond of Addie, already thinking of her as a potential stepmother. He didn't want to slow things down. He wanted to accelerate them, bring Addie into their lives even more, but he had to think of what would be best for Mary.

"'—such an incredible opportunity,'' he heard Addie saying and realized that he'd lost track of the conversation.

"What is?"

"This trip to Russia."

"What trip to Russia?" he asked blankly. *Who the hell was going to Russia?*

"Didn't you hear anything I just said?" she asked, laughing a little.

"I must have zoned out. Sorry. Who's going to Russia?"

"My father. And maybe me." Her wide smile revealed her excitement. "It's not settled yet but it looks like it could happen." She went on to explain the reason behind the trip, what this could mean to her father. Threaded through it was her pleasure that her father had asked her to go with him.

Cole felt a chill creep over him as he listened. He thought of Ronald Smith's coldly patrician features, of the chill in the other man's eyes on the two occasions they'd met. He remembered everything Addie had told him about her father and thought he had a pretty good idea of what lay behind this sudden invitation.

"That's great," he said slowly when she paused to take a breath.

"It's a wonderful opportunity," Addie said, oblivious to the flatness of his response. "I know travel has opened up a great deal in recent years but it's not always easy to get permission to visit all the—"

"For whom?" Cole interrupted.

"What?" Addie looked at him, suddenly aware that he wasn't exactly sharing her excitement.

"You said it was a wonderful opportunity. For whom?"

"I... Well, for my father, of course," she stammered, thrown off balance. "This will be a chance to look at research that's new to him. He could find data to support his theories, perhaps artifacts not known in the West."

"So why are you going?"

"I told you. I'm going to assist him. He says my help could be very valuable."

The pride in her voice made Cole grit his teeth. He wanted to grab her and shake her and tell her that her father was using her. She was so pleased about this offer to take her to Russia. Couldn't she see what was really behind it?

"Do you speak or read Russian?" he asked casually.

"No. I pointed that out to him, but he just said that the skills are still there."

"Sure they are. But I would think he'd be better off with an assistant who spoke the language."

"I imagine he'll be able to hire someone once we get there."

"Probably." He picked up the spatula they'd used to lift the pizza from the box and used the side of it to neaten the exposed edge of leftover pizza. "Has he ever asked you to travel with him before?"

"No." Addie frowned. "I used to ask him to take me with him but he never would."

"Don't you wonder why he's asking you now?" Cole asked as gently as he could.

"What do you mean?" Her frown deepened. "I assume he's asking me now because he needs me."

"But why now, Addie?"

She looked across the table at him. He thought he saw a trace of uneasiness in her eyes. Her soft mouth tightened subtly. "Why are you asking me all these questions?"

"It just seems a little odd that, after all these years, your father should suddenly decide that he can't do without you."

"I don't see anything odd about it," she said stubbornly, but he saw the flicker of doubt. "He thinks I could be helpful to him on this trip. Therefore, he's asked me to go with him."

"Couldn't you have been helpful on other trips?"

Addie laughed uneasily. "I guess so, but what does that have to do with this trip?"

"How long do you think you'll be gone?" Cole asked, sidestepping her question.

"I don't know. A few weeks. Maybe longer." Her voice slowed and she stared across the table at him, realizing for the first time what accepting her father's invitation could mean to her relationship with Cole.

He looked at her. "I don't think your father cares much for our relationship. Maybe he figures this is as good a way as any to end it."

"That's ridiculous." But even as she said it, she remembered her father's questions about her relationship with Cole and his less than pleased expression when she'd said that she hoped it was serious. It hurt to think that there might be an ulterior motive behind his invitation. That pain put a sharp edge to her voice when she continued.

"I think you're wrong about why he's asking me to go." She chuckled, the sound completely without humor. "Even if he didn't like the fact that we're seeing each other, I doubt if he'd go to so much trouble to put a stop to it. After all, it's not as if there's anything... permanent between us."

The words fell like stones into a pool of silence, ripples from their impact spreading outward to fill the room. Cole heard the question in her voice and he knew what she was waiting for him to say. All it would take was three simple words. *I love you.* Or only two. *Marry me.* She loved him. She hadn't said the words but they were in her eyes when she looked at him. If he told her he didn't want her to go with her father because he loved her and didn't want to be apart from her, she wouldn't go. It was that simple. And that complicated.

What right did he have to ask her to stay in Santa Barbara when he couldn't make her any promises? Not yet. Not until he was sure his daughter wasn't going to end up getting hurt. And only time would give him the answer to that question.

Addie heard what he didn't say and felt a tiny crack open up in her heart. There had been times during the past couple of weeks when she'd almost started to think he might love her. She didn't actually *believe* it, but she'd thought it just might be possible.

But his silence made it clear that she'd been wrong. He had to know how she felt about him; had to know that all it would take is a single word from him for her to abandon a lifetime dream and say no to her father's offer. Whatever closeness she and her father might achieve at this late date in their lives, it could never compare to what she'd almost started to believe she could have with Cole. But it looked as if she'd been wrong about that, too.

She looked away from him, her eyes a little blind as she glanced at the clock. "I didn't realize it was so late. I should be getting home," she said as if worried that she might be late for an upcoming appointment.

"Addie—"

"I guess I'd better change," she said, interrupting him ruthlessly. She tugged the lapels of his bathrobe closer around her throat, feeling suddenly underdressed. The legs of her chair scraped across the floor as she pushed back from the table and stood. She didn't look at Cole. If there was pity in his eyes, she didn't want to see it.

"Addie, I want—"

"You know, if you'd rather not drive me home, I don't mind calling a cab," she said brightly.

"I'll drive you home."

"It's so late," she protested, edging toward the door. "I really wouldn't mind taking a cab."

"I'll take you home!" he snapped.

"If you're sure."

"I'm sure."

''I won't be long, then.'' She cast him a quick, meaningless little smile, her eyes focusing somewhere over his left shoulder, and then ducked out the door.

Cole sat at the table, staring at the congealed remains of the pizza and wondering if he hadn't just made the biggest mistake of his life.

Chapter 12

Addie let herself into her father's house and closed the door behind her. Leaning back against the solid panel, she tried to shut out the sound of Cole's truck driving away.

Stupid, stupid, stupid. The word repeated itself over and over again in her head, but she wasn't sure whether to apply it to herself or only to the folly she'd committed by letting herself dream something impossible. A small, stubborn part of her insisted that it wasn't impossible, that Cole *did* care for her. And maybe that proved just how stupid she was, she thought as she pushed herself away from the door. Because if he cared for her, he would have said something.

Somewhere inside, she thought her heart might be broken, but the past few hours had contained so many emotional ups and downs that all she felt at the moment was a kind of emotional torpor. She was drained of all feeling, numb all the way to her soul. Maybe when the numbness wore off, she'd be able to sort out what she was feeling.

She had just put her foot on the bottom stair when she noticed that the light was still on in her father's den. He sometimes worked late if things were going particularly well. On impulse, she changed her mind and turned toward that light. She couldn't have said just why she wanted to see him. Maybe it was the fact that Cole's questions had lingered in her mind. Even though she was afraid of the answers, she felt compelled to seek them out.

Her father was sitting at his desk, a yellow legal tablet in front of him. When Addie stepped into the doorway, she could hear the faint scratch of his fountain pen as it slid over the paper. Her father had a deep respect for the benefits of computers, but for the first draft of his books, he preferred a legal tablet and the fountain pen he'd used for as long as she could remember. Once the first draft was done, Addie would input it into the computer and then he would do revisions on the screen.

Unaware of her presence, he continued to work and Addie took the opportunity to study him. He was getting older, she realized, feeling an odd little start of surprise. For the first time she noticed the silver that threaded through his dark hair. And there were lines in his face she hadn't seen before. He was still a handsome, distinguished man, but he was no longer a young man.

"Father?"

He didn't start with surprise when she spoke. He simply looked up from what he was doing. It occurred to her that she couldn't ever remember seeing him surprised. Or wildly excited or laughing heartily. In fact, she couldn't remember ever seeing him display a strong emotion. He was always so cool and controlled. All her life she'd admired that control, wished she could emulate it. But she found herself thinking of Cole's grin, of the blatant love in his eyes when he looked at his daughter, and she suddenly wondered if being always in control was such an admirable trait after all.

"Adelaide. I wasn't sure whether or not to expect you home tonight," he said with a glance at the brass desk clock. He didn't seem disturbed by the idea that she might be sleeping with Cole.

"Yes, well, here I am," she said with a quick little smile.

He didn't return her smile but only continued to watch her, his expression unreadable. The silence stretched. Addie told herself to say good-night and go to bed. Instead, she found herself walking farther into the den.

"Was there something you wanted?" her father asked, raising one brow in question.

"I wanted to ask you something." She set her hand on the back of a chair. The leather felt cold beneath her palm. "Earlier this evening, you asked me if I'd join you on this trip you're planning. I...wondered why."

"Why?" His brow quirked higher. "I believe I told you why."

"You told me that you thought I might be able to help you."

"That's right."

"But, you've never taken me with you on any of your other trips." She struggled to keep a note of little girl wistfulness out of her voice as she thought of all the times she'd been left behind. "Why this trip? Why now?"

He picked up the cap to his pen and set it in place, the faint click as it settled into position clearly audible in the quiet room. Moving with deliberation, he set the pen down, arranging it neatly along the top edge of the pad, which he slid to one side before clasping his hands together on the desktop. Only then did he look at her.

"Perhaps you could tell me why you're asking me these questions?" he suggested calmly.

He might have looked just the same if he were dealing with an importunate graduate student, Addie thought. The polite inquiry underlain by a faint impatience, radiating a subtle awareness that he had more important things to do. But she wasn't a grad student come to beg for his sage advice. Addie's fingers curled into a fist on the back of the chair. She was his daughter and that ought to count for something, dammit!

"Are you asking me to go with you because you're hoping to end my relationship with Cole Walker?" she asked baldly.

Surprise flickered across his face but whether at the bluntness of her question or the fact that she was asking it at all, Addie couldn't begin to guess. Just as she'd never been able to guess anything of what he was thinking.

"I assume he suggested as much?" he asked after a moment.

"Yes." She couldn't force out more than the single word.

"Interesting." He leaned forward a little and the desk lamp cast sharp shadows across his face.

"Is it true?"

"I don't think he's a particularly good influence on you," he said, avoiding a direct answer.

"So you were hoping that if I were gone for a few weeks, I'd forget about him? Or perhaps he'd forget about me?"

"Either way." He shrugged lightly. "I thought it would be best."

"For whom?" Addie was vaguely aware that she was echoing Cole's question to her. "Best for me? Or best for you?"

"Why, for you, of course." He lifted both brows in faint surprise. "I won't deny that I wouldn't care to have to train a new research assistant. The idea of having to work with a stranger holds no appeal. But naturally, my main concern is for you."

"Did it occur to you that I might be in love with Cole? That I might be very hurt if our relationship came to an end?"

"I realized that you might think you were in love with him. But you're young and you've no need to rush into anything."

Addie stared at him, feeling a curious emptiness inside. "I'm twenty-seven years old," she said almost gently. "Not exactly a child by anyone's standards."

"I didn't say that you were a child. Simply that you were young enough to fall in and out of love several more times before finding someone with whom you can spend the rest of your life."

She was silent for a moment, considering him. "Do you love me, Father?"

"What?" For once he was thrown off balance, his expression startled.

"It's a simple question. Do you love me?"

"I... Well, naturally. You're my child. Of course I... love you."

She couldn't ever remember hearing him sound so uncertain. But then she couldn't ever remember hearing him talk about love, either. Of course, why would he discuss something he'd never felt? And she was starting to think that he hadn't felt love, not real love. Not even for his work. He felt pride and satisfaction, but not a deep, passionate love—not for anyone or anything.

Addie waited for the pain, waited for the shattered sense of disillusionment to sweep over her, but it didn't happen. All she felt was a kind of sad acceptance, a vague regret for what could have been had he been a different person. And mixed in with those emotions was a deep-seated relief that it wasn't her fault that he didn't love her. He simply couldn't.

"I hope you understand that I'm acting in your best interests," he said, eyeing her a bit uneasily.

"Of course." She knew later she'd be astounded by her own calm acceptance of reality. "But I don't think I'll be going on this trip with you. I appreciate the offer, but I think you'll be better off with another assistant, one who speaks the language perhaps." She glanced around the den and suddenly realized that she didn't want to be here anymore. Not in this room, not in this house. It was an incredibly freeing thought.

"Is it because of Walker?" he asked, a faint stiffness in his voice the only sign of emotion.

"Not entirely." And that was true. She didn't even know if she and Cole *had* a relationship after tonight. They hadn't spoken three words to each other when he drove her home. But whether Cole was in her life or not, she'd just realized that she would never *have* a life as long as she stayed in this house, hoping for a miracle to occur and for her father to suddenly become a man he could never be.

"I think I'm going up to bed now," she said. "I hope I haven't interrupted you too much."

Addie felt him watching her as she left the room, but she didn't doubt that, while he might be momentarily disturbed by their conversation, he'd soon be back at work. He was too disciplined to allow anything to distract him for long.

She tried to sort out her feelings as she climbed the stairs to her room. There was pain, though not from her conversation with her father. She'd come away from that with a vague sadness and an overriding feeling of relief that there wasn't anything wrong with

her. The pain had started earlier, while she was sitting
at Cole's kitchen table, a cold pizza in front of her and
his dark eyes watching her while he didn't say the
words that would have made everything all right.

But she didn't want to think about that right now.
It was after one o'clock in the morning. The emotional turmoil of the past few hours had left her
drained and exhausted. She wanted to hang on to this
numbness for a little while, just long enough to get
some sleep. Things would look different in the morning. And even if they didn't, she'd be better able to
cope with them.

Despite the clear good sense of that thought—or
perhaps because of it—no one was more astonished
than she was when she tumbled into bed and fell almost immediately asleep.

Addie would have preferred to sleep at least around
the clock. The longer she slept, the longer she could
put off dealing with everything that had happened.
But unfortunately, she woke at dawn. Even more un-
fortunate, as far as she was concerned, was the fact
that she wasn't granted even a moment of pleasant
oblivion. She woke to instant awareness of everything
that had happened the night before.

Cole.

The hurt lodged in her chest so painfully that Addie found herself sitting up and swinging her legs over
the side of the bed, as if she could somehow run from
it. But there was no running from this hurt.

It wasn't as if he'd broken any promises, she reminded herself as she stood up. Her robe lay draped

across the foot of the bed. She picked it up and slid her arms into the sleeves, belting the thick rose-colored chenille about her waist, drawing comfort from its warmth and softness. Cole had never said or even implied that he loved her. Unless you counted the way he sometimes looked at her as if he thought she was beautiful, or the tenderness in his touch when he held her.

Don't be an idiot, Addie. You can't make promises out of a look or a touch. It was probably all in your imagination anyway.

But Nikki and Kelsey both thought he cared, she argued with herself. And if he didn't care for her, he wouldn't have brought her into Mary's life, would he?

But if he did care, why didn't he say something last night?

She had no answers to any of her questions. Nothing but an empty feeling in the pit of her stomach. Maybe she'd overreacted to his silence. Maybe she'd made an issue out of something that wasn't an issue at all. Maybe it was foolish to even think about him making a commitment of any kind. It felt as if they'd known each other forever but it hadn't really been all that long. Maybe he just needed more time.

There was scant comfort in the thought. *She* knew what was in her heart. If Cole didn't feel the same way about her now, what was to say he ever would? Addie walked restlessly around the room. She would have given a great deal to be able to escape the endless round of questions that spun through her thoughts.

Stopping by the window, she stared out at the gray, rain-soaked landscape. Last night's drizzle had disappeared but the sky was still heavily overcast, threatening more rain. Her room was at the front of the house, the window looked out on the manicured expanse of lawn and neatly clipped hedges. She stared unseeingly at the damp greenery, thinking that the landscaping was as tightly controlled and unappealing as the rest of the house. Why had she stayed here all these years?

But the question skittered out of her mind when her eyes fell on the truck parked at the curb, a familiar, slightly timeworn red truck. Cole. Her heart thudded against her breastbone as she leaned her forehead against the cold glass. It had to be Cole. But why on earth would he be sitting out there at dawn?

Addie stared at the truck, her heart beating so hard that she felt dizzy and breathless. What was he doing here? He must be waiting to see her. But why? It had to be something important for him to park out there before dawn. What could it be? Her teeth worried her lower lip for a moment before she turned away from the window. There was only one way to get an answer.

She let herself out the front door and hurried across the lawn. She hadn't thought to put on shoes and the grass was cold and wet under her feet. But she barely noticed. All her attention was focused on the truck and the solitary figure inside.

The passenger window rolled down as she approached and Cole leaned across the seat to look out at her.

"What are you doing here?" she asked, peering through the open window. "Is something wrong?"

"No. Yes." He stopped and drew a deep breath. "I wanted to talk to you. Would you please get in the truck?"

"I... It's early, Cole. I'm not even dressed yet." Addie gave him a quick, meaningless smile. She didn't want to talk to him, not if it meant opening up wounds that hadn't even begun to heal. It was too soon and too much had happened. She needed time.

"Please." The simple word held more power than she'd have thought possible.

"Just for a moment," she said reluctantly.

She opened the truck door and slid into the passenger seat. Cole hit the button to roll up the window, closing them into the quiet interior. Addie sat as close to the door as she could without being obvious about it.

"How long have you been sitting here?" she asked when he seemed willing to let the silence build.

"I don't know. A couple of hours, I guess." Cole frowned and ran his fingers through his hair. From the rumpled look of the dark gold waves, it wasn't the first time he'd made the gesture. His jaw was darkened by a day's growth of beard and there were shadows under his eyes. He looked as if he hadn't slept all night and Addie was startled to find herself actually hoping he hadn't. She hadn't realized she had such a vengeful streak. But then, she was learning all kinds of new things about herself lately.

"What did you want to talk to me about?" she asked.

"I wanted to apologize."

"For what?" *For not loving me?* she thought painfully. He hardly owed her an apology for that.

"For what I said about your father, about his reasons for asking you to go on this trip with him."

"You were right about why he asked me to go with him," Addie said after a moment. She didn't look at him, staring out the window at the rain-washed landscape instead. "He thought my being gone for a while would put an end to our relationship. I actually thought he might finally be anxious to get to know me." Her mouth twisted in a painful smile. "More fool I."

"I'm sorry," Cole said simply, and she knew he meant it.

"Me, too." She sighed, thinking of all the hurt she could have saved herself if she'd faced the truth about her father a long time ago. But then she shook herself mentally. What was done was done and she wasn't going to waste yet more time in regrets.

"That's not all I wanted to apologize for," Cole said, breaking into her thoughts.

"You didn't have to apologize for that, let alone anything else."

"Actually, I do. There are things I *didn't* say last night that I regret more than the ones I did."

Addie had a sudden, horrible fear that he was going to try to explain why he didn't love her. She reached for the door handle. "I can't imagine what you mean," she said hastily. "Really, you don't owe me any apologies for anything."

"Please, Addie. Let me explain." Cole set his hand on her arm. She felt the light touch burn through the fabric of her robe, sinking under her skin and filling her with a longing so powerful that her body ached with it.

"Cole, I—"

"Please." Once again, she couldn't deny the simple plea.

"All right." She let her hand drop from the handle, sitting rigidly in her seat. "I'll listen."

"Thank you." But he didn't continue immediately. When she stole a glance at his face, she thought he might be trying to sort out his thoughts. "Last night, there were things I didn't say that I should have. Things about our relationship, about my... feelings. I told myself I was worried about Mary, that I couldn't say anything to you until I was sure she wasn't going to get hurt."

"She's your daughter and you love her," Addie said a bit wistfully.

"Yes, I do, but she's a bit too small for me to hide behind."

"What do you mean?" She looked at his face for the first time since getting into the truck and what she saw there made her heart beat faster. Remembering the hurt she'd felt last night, she struggled to rein in the hope rising inside her.

"I *was* worried about Mary getting hurt, but when I thought about it, I realized that I was just as worried about myself." Cole's tone was self-condemning.

"Why were you worried about yourself?" Addie asked, bewildered.

"That I'd make another mistake. That I'd... be alone again." He reached out and caught her hand, his fingers holding hers a little too tight for comfort. Addie didn't complain. She didn't even notice.

"When my first marriage broke up, I felt relief as much as anything else. Roxie and I did okay together as long as it was just the two of us. I was doing stunt work and I'd just started flying. I was making a decent amount of money and she was pulling in enough work as an actress to make us more than comfortable."

"I didn't know she was an actress," Addie exclaimed. Her heart sank a little. The word "actress" conjured up images of beauty and glamour with which she could never hope to compete. "Was she... beautiful?"

"Roxie?" Cole frowned a little, looking back down the years and trying to conjure up his ex-wife's image. "Not really. She was..." He paused, groping for the right word to describe her. "Lively," he said finally. "You tended to forget that she wasn't particularly pretty because she kind of sparkled."

Lively. Sparkling. Addie felt her heart sink still more. She'd almost rather have heard that Roxie had been a raving beauty.

"Anyway, we did okay," Cole continued. His thumb moved absently over the back of her hand. "I don't know that we were ever madly in love, but we were attracted to one another and, somehow, getting married seemed like a good idea. If Roxie hadn't gotten pregnant with Mary, I suppose we might have stayed married quite a while longer."

"Didn't she want a baby?"

"About as much as she wanted a hole in the head," Cole said ruefully.

"I suppose pregnancy is a real concern to an actress, ruining her figure and all." Addie didn't know why she felt the need to try to be charitable toward the other woman.

Cole shook his head. "Roxie wasn't worried about her figure or even all that much about her career. She just flat didn't want to be a mother. She didn't particularly like kids, never cooed over babies in the supermarket and never wanted to have any of her own."

"But you felt differently," Addie prompted when he stopped.

"Yeah. From the moment I found out about the baby, I wanted it. I'd never given much thought to being a father until then, but there was never a doubt in my mind that I wanted that child. I asked her to have it and she agreed." He lifted one shoulder in a half shrug. "We both knew the marriage was over, either way. If she had the baby, she wouldn't want to stay. And if she didn't have it, I couldn't have stayed."

"So she had Mary and gave her to you and left," Addie summed up quietly. She'd expected to despise Mary's mother, to condemn her for abandoning her child. Instead she found herself, if not understanding the choices Roxie had made, at least respecting them. At least she'd left Mary in loving care. Maybe she'd been indifferent to that fact but Addie preferred to believe that she'd cared for her child at least that much.

"She gave me sole custody and walked away without regret," Cole agreed. He stared down at their linked hands, frowning a little. "I didn't think I had any regrets, either. And I don't. Not about Roxie. But I spent a lot of time thinking about it last night and I realized that I've got a few more scars than I'd realized."

"I doubt if a marriage can break up without leaving scars," Addie said.

"Maybe not. But I didn't notice them before. For the first couple of years I was so busy figuring out how to be a father that I didn't have time to even think about the divorce. All I could think about was that Mary was totally dependent on me to do the right things for her."

"Mary's heart condition must have made it even more difficult."

"It didn't help," he admitted with what she suspected was massive understatement. "I guess by the time I came up for air and started dating again, I thought I'd put the divorce behind me, worked through whatever I was supposed to work through and was ready to go on with my life. Until I met you, nothing happened to make me think otherwise."

"Me?"

Addie gave him a startled look and Cole's smile took on a rueful edge. She didn't have the faintest idea of how she'd turned his life upside down. He shifted his hold on her hand, his thumb brushing against the inside of her wrist, feeling her pulse jump at his touch. The small, involuntary betrayal gave him hope. Maybe he hadn't screwed up too badly last night. Maybe they could salvage things.

"I realized last night that I was scared to death of you."

"Me?" she said again, her voice rising on an incredulous note.

"You."

"How on earth could you be scared of me?" Addie asked in bewilderment. "I'm about as frightening as...as that tree over there," she said, gesturing to a leafless sweet gum across the street.

"I'd probably find that tree pretty scary if I found myself falling in love with it."

Addie stared at him, her eyes wide with shock. Once, when she was a little girl, she'd fallen from the top of a jungle gym. She hadn't sustained any lasting injuries but she'd hit the ground hard enough to knock the air out of her lungs. Twenty years later she felt much the same way she'd felt then—the same feeling of breathlessness, the almost achy feeling in her chest.

"What did you say?" Her voice sounded a little faint and far away, but it was surprisingly steady.

"I love you." The words were stark, unadorned. She couldn't possibly have mistaken what he was saying. "I love you and it scares me to death."

"Oh, my." Addie groped for a more intelligent response. There had to be something else to say. Like maybe that she loved him, too, and was at least as scared as he was. But Cole was still speaking.

"I didn't care much when Roxie left because I'd realized that I didn't really love her. I didn't like seeing my marriage fail, but it wasn't a personal kind of hurt, if that makes any sense."

He paused and Addie nodded obediently. She only half understood what he was saying. But that was okay. She could make him repeat it all later when she could think again.

"If something happened . . . if you left me—" Cole broke off, his hands tightening almost painfully around hers. "I don't think I'd know how to deal with that. I love you so much."

"Oh."

One side of Cole's mouth kicked upward. Maybe her response wasn't exactly what he'd dreamed of, but the look in her eyes was. One of the things he loved about her was the way her eyes revealed what she was thinking, what she was feeling. And the way she was looking at him now was melting the ice from around his heart and telling him that everything was going to be all right.

"Is that all you're going to say?" he asked softly. "Just 'oh'?"

"I think so," she said after a moment's consideration.

"You don't think you could find something else to say?" His hands slid up her forearms, slipping under the wide sleeves of her robe.

"Only that I love you so much it hurts," she said, rushing the words out.

Cole felt as if a huge weight had rolled from his shoulders. He'd seen the answer in her eyes but he'd needed to hear the words to be sure that everything was going to be all right.

"I want you to marry me," he said, tugging her toward him.

"Oh." The word was soft and breathy. Cole's smile widened into a grin. He felt happiness well up inside him, making his chest ache.

"Is that a yes?"

"Yes."

"Are you only going to speak in monosyllables from now on?"

"Maybe." Addie felt dizzy with happiness. She smiled up at him, her heart in her eyes.

"If I could, I'd carry you off to Las Vegas and we'd get married today, but I want to give Mary plenty of time to get used to the idea. She likes you already and I know she'd like to have a mother, but I don't want to— What's wrong?" he asked as tears welled up in Addie's eyes.

"I'm just so happy. You and Mary. I've never been part of a real family."

"Well, when you marry into the Walker clan, you get plenty of family. In fact, you'll probably get pretty sick of us after a while."

"Never." She put her hands on his shoulders and leaned closer, only to be frustrated by the console between the seats.

"I picked a hell of a place to propose," Cole said with a half laugh.

"It's perfect." It could have been a coal bin and she'd still have thought it perfect. As long as he was looking at her like that, it didn't matter where they were. She set her fingertips against his cheek, reveling in the freedom to touch him, the knowledge that he was hers, now and forever. "I love you," she whispered, tasting the joy the words gave her.

"I love you," he said softly.

And nothing else in the world mattered.

*   *   *   *   *

*Look for Dallas Schulze's
Harlequin Historical,
SHORT STRAW BRIDE,
coming in November 1996!*

In April 1997
Bestselling Author

DALLAS SCHULZE

takes her Family Circle series to new heights with

TESSA'S CHILD

In April 1997 Dallas Schulze brings readers a
brand-new, longer, out-of-series title featuring the
characters from her popular Family Circle miniseries.

When rancher Keefe Walker found Tessa Wyndham he
knew that she needed a man's protection—she was
pregnant, alone and on the run from a heartless past.
Keefe was also hiding from a dark past...but in one
overwhelming moment he and Tessa forged a family
bond that could never be broken.

Available in April wherever books are sold.

DSST

The exciting new cross-line continuity series about love,
marriage—and Daddy's unexpected need for a baby
carriage!

It all began with *THE BABY NOTION*
by Dixie Browning (Desire #1011 7/96)

And the romance in New Hope, Texas, continues with:

BABY IN A BASKET
by Helen R. Myers (Romance #1169 8/96)

Confirmed bachelor Mitch McCord finds a baby on
his doorstep and turns to lovely gal-next-door
Jenny Stevens for some lessons in fatherhood—and love!

Don't miss the upcoming books in this wonderful series:

MARRIED...WITH TWINS!
by Jennifer Mikels (Special Edition#1054, 9/96)

HOW TO HOOK A HUSBAND (AND A BABY)
by Carolyn Zane (Yours Truly #29, 10/96)

DISCOVERED: DADDY
by Marilyn Pappano (Intimate Moments #746, 11/96)

DADDY KNOWS LAST continues
each month...only from

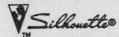

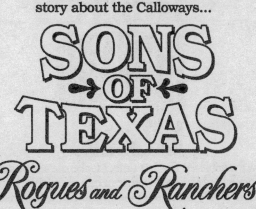
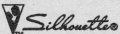

FORTUNE'S Children™

Bestselling Author
LISA JACKSON

Continues the twelve-book series—FORTUNE'S CHILDREN
in August 1996 with Book Two

THE MILLIONAIRE AND THE COWGIRL

When playboy millionaire Kyle Fortune inherited a Wyoming
ranch from his grandmother, he never expected to come
face-to-face with Samantha Rawlings, the willful woman
he'd never forgotten...and the daughter he'd never known.
Although Kyle enjoyed his jet-setting life-style, Samantha and
Caitlyn made him yearn for hearth and home.

MEET THE FORTUNES—a family whose legacy is greater than
riches. Because where there's a will...there's a *wedding!*

*A CASTING CALL TO
ALL FORTUNE'S CHILDREN FANS!*
If you are truly one of the fortunate
few, you may win a trip to
Los Angeles to audition for
Wheel of Fortune®. Look for
details in all retail Fortune's Children titles!

WHEEL of FORTUNE®

Look us up on-line at: http://www.romance.net

FC-2-C-R

You can run, but you cannot
hide...from love.

This August, experience danger, excitement and
love on the run with three couples thrown
together by life-threatening circumstances.

Enjoy three complete stories by some of your
favorite authors—all in one special collection!

THE PRINCESS AND THE PEA
by Kathleen Korbel

IN SAFEKEEPING
by Naomi Horton

FUGITIVE
by Emilie Richards

Available this August wherever books are sold.

Look us up on-line at:http://www.romance.net

SREQ0896

If you are looking for more titles by

DALLAS SCHULZE

Don't miss this chance to order additional stories by
one of Silhouette's most popular authors:

Silhouette Intimate Moments®

#07377	THE BABY BARGAIN	$3.25	☐
#07462	THE HELL-RAISER	$3.39	☐
#07500	SECONDHAND HUSBAND	$3.50	☐
#07608	A VERY CONVENIENT MARRIAGE	$3.50 U.S.	☐
		$3.99 CAN.	☐

(limited quantities available on certain titles)

TOTAL AMOUNT	$
POSTAGE & HANDLING	$
($1.00 for one book, 50¢ for each additional)	
APPLICABLE TAXES*	$_____
TOTAL PAYABLE	$_____

(Send check or money order—please do not send cash)

To order, complete this form and send it, along with a check or money order
for the total above, payable to Silhouette Books, to: **In the U.S.:** 3010 Walden
Avenue, P.O. Box 9077, Buffalo, NY 14269-9077; **In Canada:** P.O. Box 636,
Fort Erie, Ontario, L2A 5X3.

Name:_____

Address:_____ City:_____

State/Prov.:_____ Zip/Postal Code:_____

*New York residents remit applicable sales taxes.
 Canadian residents remit applicable GST and provincial taxes.   SDSBACK4